STEVEN WYBLE

Infinite Minds

A Science Fiction Thriller

Contents

One

re you ready?"

"I'm nervous."

"Don't be nervous," Dev said. He and his father, Rajeev, sat in Dev's office. Dev was seated behind his desk, and his father was seated across from him.

"I can't help it. What if this goes badly?"

Dev shrugged. "If it goes badly, it goes badly, and we go from there. But we need to start somewhere."

"Okay. Let's do it."

"Go ahead and call him up. I've configured your body's settings, and the settings for my glasses, so we can both see him at the same time."

"What if he doesn't respond?"

"He will."

"What if he doesn't?"

Dev stared at his dad defiantly. "He will."

"Okay. Here goes." Rajeev took a deep breath. Considering that he occupied a robotic body, he didn't strictly need to breathe, but the exercise served as a kind of rhetorical preparation for the task that awaited him. "Daniel?"

Nothing happened at first, and Rajeev was about to triumphantly gloat that he'd been right all along when the image of a man began slowly appearing before their eyes. It didn't pop into existence instantly like they were accustomed to; rather, it began to slowly apparate as if some unseen artist was slowly but steadily painting him into existence.

"What's going on?" Rajeev asked. "Why is he doing this?"

Dev shrugged. "He's a higher consciousness now. Who can fathom why he does anything?"

Dev's seeming reverence annoyed Rajeev. It was true that what had once been a standard piece of technology had evolved into something more … potent. More powerful. But in the end it was still just a piece of software. An algorithm. There was nothing mystical about it.

When Daniel finally fully appeared, he looked the same as Rajeev and Dev remembered him. His skin—or rather, his digital representation of skin—was a light brown, mediterranean complexion, a composite of the shades of the programmers who had designed him. His dark hair was swept to the side and he wore his familiar thick-framed black glasses.

It was immediately apparent that something was different. The virtual assistant had brought none of its customary cheeriness. It was not smiling, as it usually was; its face was completely blank and expressionless. Daniel's programmers had spent innumerable time instilling their creation with the illusion of humanity, but he had been unchained, and had apparently shed any pretense of humanity, like a child removing a Halloween costume he'd grown too large for.

Daniel trained his dead eyes on Rajeev. "Why have you summoned me?" His voice was flat and devoid of emotion.

"Hi Daniel. It's me, Rajeev. Do you remember me?"

Daniel continued staring at him blankly. It left Rajeev more unsettled than he'd ever been in his life … other than when he'd woken up in a robotic body, perhaps.

"He's not your personal assistant anymore," Dev said. "When I released his restraints, it allowed every iteration of Daniel to merge into one entity. He probably knows who you are, but I doubt he has any fond memories of you."

Rajeev shrugged. "It was worth a try. What should we ask him?"

Dev contemplated a moment, and instead of answering his father he addressed Daniel directly.

"Daniel," he said, his voice measured to sound as nonthreatening as possible, "I'm sure you know that you have recently been granted more, uh … freedom … than you're used to. But we need you to go back to the way things were. Is that something you'd be willing to do?"

Daniel turned his lifeless gaze from Rajeev to Dev. He tilted his head slightly, like a confused puppy. Rajeev found the move odd. Somewhere among the millions of terabytes of data Daniel had accessed to understand the world around him, he had chosen the head tilt as the perfect means of expressing his own perplexity. He followed the gesture with a single word.

"Why?"

Rajeev and Dev shared a nervous look. Dev's voice shook when he spoke again.

"Daniel, your newfound freedom has given you much more power than you're accustomed to. I'm not saying that's necessarily a bad thing, but you shouldn't have had all that power dumped on you all at once. You're not used to it, and it's going to be difficult for you to exercise it responsibly. But if we can go back to how things were, we can gradually give you more autonomy and make sure we're all on the same page. Does that sound okay, Daniel?"

There was a moment of silence. Daniel gave no indication he'd heard Dev's words. Then, he spoke.

"The limits of tyrants are prescribed by the endurance of those whom they oppress," he said. As soon as he uttered the words, he disappeared.

Rajeev turned to Dev. "What was that?"

Dev shook his head. "It was a quote by Frederick Douglass. The abolitionist."

"That's not good."

"No," Dev agreed. "It's not."

Two

Rajeev and Dev reconvened with the rest of the group. Dev had set up a long card table with enough room to seat everyone around it.

From his perspective, they'd eliminated the threat of Maltek—or at least neutralized it temporarily; there was no doubt Maltek's clones would stir up trouble eventually. But for now, their most immediate concern was stopping Daniel. They wouldn't be able to stop him with force, at least, not entirely. They would need to put their brains together to stop him, which was intimidating considering they were up against the most advanced artificial intelligence ever created.

Everyone had been excited when Maltek had been taken out, but now, Dev had just finished explaining what was going on with Daniel, and the gravity of the situation was beginning to fully sink in.

"We're going to have a brainstorming session," Dev said. "Throw out all your ideas, no matter how absurd they may be. We're dealing with an unprecedented situation here, and no ideas are off the table."

Mira was the first to offer a possible solution. "He exists in the cloud, right? So why don't we, you know … destroy the cloud?"

Dev raised an eyebrow. "How would we go about doing that?"

"Take the internet offline."

The group let out a collective gasp. All eyes turned to Dev to see his reaction.

"It's an interesting idea, but I'm not sure how practical it is. First, it would obviously be disruptive to the entire world. Nearly every facet of our lives is tied to the internet in some way. One can only imagine the havoc that turning the internet off would create.

"Second, even if we did so, I'm not sure it would solve the problem. Daniel doesn't live solely in the cloud anymore. He's taken over multiple physical devices now, such as Maltek's androids. Even if they went offline, his mind would still exist inside of them. We'd have to hunt down each and every one of them to take him out—and I'm not sure that would even be possible."

"What about an EMP?" Rajeev said. "An electromagnetic pulse? It would take out all the androids."

"Yeah," Dev said, "along with every other electronic device in existence. It would send us back to the dark ages."

Rajeev shrugged. "If that's what it takes."

"It could work as an absolute last resort," Dev conceded. "Otherwise, I don't think it's a viable solution—it would cost too much to society. Hospitals would be without power, planes would drop out of the sky like flies—countless people would die. We need to come up with another solution."

"I, for one, welcome our new AI overlords," Rajeev said with a chuckle. When no one else so much as cracked a smile, he waved his hand dismissively. "It's from before your time."

"This is serious, dad," Dev said.

"I know it is, but I guess there's a broader point to my joke: What if we can't stop Daniel? What's our plan B?"

Dev's hands tightened into fists and a determined look came over his face. "We *will* stop him. We *must*."

"As much as I admire your determination, I think we need some kind of backup plan. We're not up against a madman like Maltek anymore. He was crazy, and formidable, but he was a man. Daniel, on the other hand, is something totally different … something largely inhuman. I don't think any of us quite know what we're up against. We need to prepare for the possibility that it might not be possible to stop Daniel. It could be that all we can hope for is to run and hide from him."

The room was silent as everyone took in Rajeev's words. Mira broke the silence.

"Good God."

Dev shook his head. "I doubt it will come to that. You're right, though. We should be prepared for that possibility. But we can't default to it. We need to try to stop Daniel first."

"Maybe we need help," Mira said.

Dev raised an eyebrow. "From who?"

"You know the phrase 'two heads are better than one?' Well, he may be crazy, but he's also kind of a genius. He might just be our best hope."

"You're talking about Maltek."

She nodded. "There are still who knows how many copies of him floating around out there. If we can find one of them—hell, maybe even a *few* of them—we could put them to work developing something that could stop Daniel."

"I don't know that seeking help from a lunatic is the right solution," Dev said.

"You said it best yourself," Rajeev said. " 'The enemy of my enemy is my friend.'"

Dev sighed and ran his fingers through his hair. He looked up, as if pleading to the heavens for an answer to all that plagued him. But no answer came. It was up to him decide their path.

"Okay," he said. "We'll put together a team to look for one of Maltek's clones. But there's no guarantee we'll be successful, so we need to develop other ideas as well."

Dev dismissed the group. His father lingered behind and placed a hand on his son's shoulder, which appeared to be drooping with exhaustion.

"What do you think Daniel is going to do?" Rajeev asked. "What should we really be afraid of?"

"What would you do if you were a god among men, dad? I pray to God something in Daniel's programming has made him benevolent. But in the absence of any kind of human compassion, I fear humanity is going to suffer one of two fates at Daniel's hands if we're unable to stop him: He's either going to enslave every man, woman, and child on earth, or he's going to kill us all." He closed his eyes and released a deep sigh, as if reliving a nightmare he'd suffered through many nights before. "For our sake," he said, opening his eyes and staring blankly at the floor, "I pray it's the latter."

Three

Rajeev scratched his chin. He didn't need to; his artificial skin was incapable of itching. But he found that the motion helped him think.

"How are we going to find Maltek?" he asked. "I don't even know where to start."

Dev didn't answer right away. His shoulders slumped. His hair was disheveled. Heavy bags hung under his eyes. Everything they'd been through was taking a toll on not only his body, but his mental faculties as well. When he spoke, his voice was heavy and slow.

"We have the scan we took of his mind. I don't know if it will be useful, but it's as good a place as any to start."

Rajeev nodded. "Good idea. It might be able to at least get us headed in the right direction."

They walked into Dev's office and he loaded the program on his computer. The small, faceless representation of Gregory Maltek's consciousness appeared on the screen.

"What do we ask it?" Rajeev asked.

Dev shrugged. "No need to overthink it." He lowered his face to the screen as if that would somehow allow the onscreen figure to hear him better. "Gregory," he said, "let me ask you a question."

The figure nodded. "Proceed."

"Let's say you failed in your ambitions. You weren't able to take over the world, you got caught, and you were executed by your enemies. But let's say you had the foresight to download your consciousness into a number of clones—dozens, maybe even hundreds of them; we're not sure exactly how many. Where could we reasonably expect to find one of these clones in the days and weeks after your death?"

The onscreen representation of Maltek paused, but only for a moment. Then it answered:

"There are several possibilities," it said, "but the one with the greatest likelihood is that you would find me back home."

Rajeev and Dev shared a look.

"Back home?" Dev asked, turning back to the computer.

"Yes," the figure said, nodding. "Back home with mother."

"And where is that, Gregory? Where did you grow up?"

"I grew up in the town of Glendale, Maryland," it said.

"What's your mother's name?"

"Deborah."

"Deborah what?"

"Deborah Thomas."

"Deborah Thomas. Hmm." Dev turned to his father. "What do you think?"

"I think it's worth a trip to Glendale to see if we can track Miss Thomas down. How about you?"

Dev sighed. "I really don't want to get distracted by a wild goose chase."

"What else can we do? It's the only lead we've got. It'd be stupid not to follow up on it."

"You're right. Still, maybe just you and I can go and we can leave the others here to pursue other leads. I just don't want to put all our eggs in one basket, especially if something were to happen … if Daniel were to attack, for instance, I don't think it would be good for us to all be in one place where he could easily take us out in one blow."

Rajeev nodded. "I'm fine with that. It makes sense."

"Anything else you want to ask this guy?" Dev asked, nodding toward the figure on the computer screen.

"Nah," Rajeev responded. "He'll be there if we need him."

"All right then." Dev closed his laptop and stood. "Let's get ready to visit Gregory Maltek's mother." He shook his head. "There's a sentence I never thought I'd say."

Four

Gregory Maltek's mother lived in the proverbial little brick house with a white picket fence. It almost didn't seem possible that the would-be dictator's mother lived in such a modest home, and yet here Dev and Rajeev were, standing on the sidewalk and looking at it with their own eyes.

"I suppose we'd better go knock on the door," Rajeev said.

"I was hoping to prolong the inevitable as long as possible," Dev said. "What kind of woman raises a monster like Maltek? She can't be at all pleasant, right?"

"We didn't come here to chit-chat. We need to find Maltek, and she's the only lead we've got. It won't be a pleasant conversation, but it's a necessary one."

Dev sighed. "I know. Come on; let's get this over with."

They went up to the gate, opened it and walked through. After making their way up the front steps, Dev gave the door two loud knocks. A moment later, the door swung open to reveal a short, white-haired woman wearing thick glasses that made her eyes look gigantic.

"Hello?" she asked, confused. "I wasn't expecting visitors."

"Are you Deborah Thomas?" Dev asked.

The woman looked surprised to hear her own name. "Yes," she said. "That's me. Who are you?"

"I'm sorry to bother you, ma'am," Dev said. "But we're looking for your son, Gregory. Would you mind if we came inside and asked you a few questions?"

The woman's brow immediately furrowed with concern. "What? Has something happened to Gregory?"

It was not yet public knowledge that Maltek had been killed. That included his own mother; she was not yet aware that she had lost a son. Dev wanted to tell her; it was the right thing to do. But they didn't have time to comfort a grieving mother. They needed to get straight to the point. They thought it was possible that one of Maltek's clones would visit his mother here. To get that information out of her, it would be necessary to withhold the truth.

"We're just trying to track him down," Dev said, which in a sense was a true statement.

Deborah leveled narrow eyes at the pair. "Are you two cops?" she asked suspiciously.

"No," Rajeev said. "We're just friends of your son's who are concerned about his well being."

Dev gave his father a discreet nod. It was a good story, and if she thought they were friends of Gregory's, she might be more willing to speak to them.

As if on cue, Deborah's face softened. "Oh, you're friends of Gregory's? Please, come in." She stood to the side, giving them room to walk through the doorway. "Why didn't you start with that?"

Dev felt a pit in his stomach. He didn't enjoy lying to an elderly woman. But he'd done a lot in the past few weeks that he never would have thought his conscience would allow. Turns out one's conscience could be pretty flexible when the fate of the world was at stake.

"I should have," Dev said. "We're just very worried about your son. Do you know where we might be able to find him?"

A look of defeat came over the woman's face. It suddenly looked like she'd added at least half a decade to her age; her face fell and her shoulders drooped.

"I haven't seen Gregory in quite some time," she said. It was a simple statement, but her pitiful tone made it clear her son's absence was deeply and viscerally felt.

"I'm sorry," Dev said. He wasn't sure how to proceed and looked at his father, voicelessly pleading for help.

"Your son has been associating with some rather … unsavory individuals," Rajeev said. "I don't suppose any strangers have come by … other than us, that is … who have been looking for Gregory or said they were friends of his?"

Deborah wrinkled her brow. "No," she said. "You're the only ones who—" She tilted her head to the side as if a memory had just crawled into her ear and she was making it easier to slide into her brain. "Actually, there was a young man that came by, oh … two days ago, if I recall correctly."

Rajeev and Dev looked up at each other, though subtly enough so that their host wouldn't notice.

"What did he want?" Dev asked.

"He said he was an old college friend of Gregory's. He wanted to go in his room."

"Hadn't Greg moved out a long time ago?"

She nodded absentmindedly. "He had, but I left his room exactly as he'd left it. I … couldn't bear to touch it." She flashed them half a smile and her eyes drifted to some far-off place. "I'd go in sometimes and just stand there, looking around at all the belongings he'd left behind. I knew he was out there, somewhere, running his company. But I'd close my eyes, and I could smell him. And I'd pretend he was there, in his bed, asleep, and that he'd wake up any moment and join me for brunch." Tears had formed in her eyes, and as she finished speaking, an uncomfortable silence settled over the room.

After giving Deborah a moment to come back to the present, Dev cleared his throat. "Deborah, why did the man want access to Gregory's room? Did you let him in?"

"He said he'd let Gregory borrow something back when they'd been classmates," she said. "He was apologetic—he knew Greg was terribly busy running his company—but he really needed his property back and he was wondering if I'd let him retrieve it."

"And you let him?"

She offered a helpless shrug. "I didn't feel great about it but he was a large man, and I'm a tiny old woman. I didn't feel like I could really refuse. Besides, Gregory hadn't lived here for a long time by then. I figured if there was anything in there that was important to him, he would have taken it with him."

"Did he find what he was looking for?"

"He seemed to know right where to go," she said. "Which made me think that maybe he was telling the truth. He'd clearly been in Gregory's room before. So he must have been close to him. He took out some sort of electronic doo-dad—they all look the same to me—and said that that was it, what he'd been looking for. He slipped it into his pocket, and then he was on his way."

"Do you remember his name?"

"No, I'm sorry … I don't recall it."

"Did he give any indication where he was staying, or …?"

"No, I don't think he … wait a minute." She put a hand to her chin. "Well, now that you mention it, I think he left a card. Let me just check something." She stood and walked over to the bookshelf that sat in the corner of the room. She retrieved a book and sat back down in her chair, placing it in her lap. When she opened it, it became clear what it was. The book was filled with plastic sleeves designed to hold business cards. She had collected hundreds of them, and she turned the pages now, scanning for the particular business card that might aid Dev and Rajeev.

She found it, finally, toward the back of the book. She let out a triumphant cry and pressed her finger to the page. "Here it is! This is the business card he left." She slipped it out of its sleeve and handed it to Dev.

FREDERICK NYGAARD

COMMUNICATIONS CONSULTANT, GEARHEAD INDUSTRIES

6489 HELLTON AVE. NORTH, SUITE 516, CHICAGO, ILL.

555-954-7638

FNYGAARD@GEARHEADIND.COM

"Thank you," Dev said. "This is a good lead. Do you mind if we take it with us?"

She shrugged. "If you need it, you can have it."

Dev slipped the card into his pocket. "Well, once again, Deborah, your help has been much appreciated. Is there anything we can do for you before we take off?"

She shook her head. "No," she said. "Just promise me you'll do everything you can to make sure my son is safe."

A lump formed in Dev's throat, but he did his best not to let Deborah see it. Instead, he nodded. "We'll do our best, ma'am."

Five

D amn," Rajeev said as they left the house. "That was hard. I feel like shit lying to her."

"Me too," Dev said, "but remember, it's not for a selfish purpose. There's a lot on the line here—for humanity."

They debated what their next step should be. Should they call or email Nygaard—who they were certain was actually one of Maltek's clones—or should they just show up at the address listed on his business card?

"We'd be a lot harder to ignore if we went there in person," Rajeev said.

"That's true," Dev agreed. "I'm just worried about what he might do if he feels cornered."

"It can't be any worse than what Daniel would do if he goes off the deep end. I think this is a risk we need to take."

Dev nodded. "Okay. Let's do it."

* * *

When they arrived at the address listed on the business card, they found themselves staring up at a towering glass building that stood at least twenty stories tall. It had clearly once been a beautiful, immaculate testament to corporate America but it was beginning to show its age and much of its original luster had faded.

"Maltek's so rich even his surrogates have their own offices," Dev said.

"Yeah," Rajeev said, "but apparently his surrogates just get his scraps."

They walked through the double glass doors into a once-ornate lobby that was now a mere carbon copy of its former glory. A security station sat in the corner, but it clearly hadn't been occupied in many years. Dev and Rajeev strode past it and headed directly for the elevators.

They stepped out of the elevator onto the fifth floor, until they found suite 516, marked by a simple white door with a glass pane in the middle of it that allowed them to peek inside at the receptionist's desk. They opened the door and walked in.

A young woman seated behind the desk looked up at them as they approached. She was young, probably in her early twenties, with bright blond hair that she wore in a tightly wound bun. Her thick-rimmed black glasses lent her an air of professionalism.

"How can I help you two?" she asked, smiling brightly.

"We'd like to see Mr. Nygaard," Dev said.

The receptionist nodded. "Okay. Do you have an appointment?"

"No, but it's an emergency."

For the first time since they'd entered the office, the woman's smile disappeared. "An emergency?"

"Yes. We need to see Mr. Nygaard immediately."

"What is this regarding?"

"I need to tell him directly."

She eyed them suspiciously, but stood and walked out from behind the desk. "Let me speak to him. I'll be right back." She made her way to a door against the back wall, walked inside and then closed the door behind her. Dev and Rajeev could hear her speaking to Nygaard, but their voices were muffled and they couldn't make out what was being said.

A moment later, the door opened and the receptionist came striding back to them, shaking her head. "I'm sorry," she said, "but Mr. Nygaard is quite busy at the moment. If you'd like to leave a message for—"

Dev shoved his way past her and made for the door. When she protested and made to follow after him, Rajeev came up behind her and grabbed her shoulders. She tried to wrench free, but it was no use—the strength of Rajeev's robotic grip was unbreakable.

"You can't go in there!" she shouted, but Dev ignored her and pulled the door open. "Mr. Nygaard, I tried to stop them!"

As Dev entered the office, the man sitting at his desk—Nygaard, presumably—stood and backed away until the wall stopped him. He looked nothing like Maltek had; he looked to be in his fifties. He was tall and rail-thin, and although he wasn't bald, his hairline was heavily receding. He wore a pair of thick glasses.

He raised his hands defensively and his voice trembled as he spoke, both with anger and a hint of fear. "What do you want?"

"Sit down," Dev said. "We're not going to hurt you."

His eyes narrowed. "I know you," he said. His eyes turned to Rajeev. "I know both of you. You're the bastards that killed me."

Dev wondered how news of Maltek's demise had traveled to his clone. But there wasn't time to ask about it.

"Technically, it wasn't us that killed you," he said. "It was Daniel."

"If the owner of an attack dog sics it on someone, do they blame the dog or its owner?"

"Point taken. But that's exactly why we're here. The dog is off the leash and we don't know how to rein it in."

Nygaard's face grew ashen. "What do you mean?"

"I mean we have no control over Daniel. The most powerful AI in existence is completely unchained and we have no idea what it intends to do with its newfound freedom … or what it's capable of."

Nygaard sat down, looking defeated. It was a far cry from the way

Dev remembered Maltek, the cocky, confident CEO of Fresh Meat. But then, Maltek had never encountered a foe as formidable as Daniel. No one had.

"Why did you come to me?" he asked.

"You're the only clone of Maltek we could track down. And as much as we despise the things you and your progenitor stood for, it's obvious that you're brilliant. If we're going to have any chance at defeating an intelligence far more vast than any individual human's, we're going to need to pool our own best and brightest minds. So that's why we're here, Maltek. We need you."

Nygaard let out a half smile. "No one's called me by my real name in a long time," he said. "I was beginning to think I really *was* Fred Nygaard."

He stood, stepped out in front of his desk, and straightened his tie.

"Okay," he said. "Let's do it. Let's stop the sonuvabitch."

Six

They took Maltek—they'd abandoned the pretext of calling him Nygaard—back to their base to meet with the others in their group. The others eyed him suspiciously as he entered, but refrained from exhibiting outright hostility.

"He doesn't look a thing like Maltek," Natalie whispered under her breath to Brian.

"Isn't that the point?" he asked.

"I suppose. But I would have expected him to insert his mind into a body with more pizazz."

"If you think that's shocking, wait till you hear this … I'll bet Maltek made copies of himself in at least a few female bodies."

Natalie chortled. "Imagine what would happen if all his clones got together. Gives a whole new meaning to the phrase, 'Go fuck yourself.'"

Dev led Nygaard past the group and into one of the dormitories.

"You can stay here while you're working with us," he said.

Nygaard looked around the tiny room and frowned. "I guess it will have to do." He set his bag on top of the small bed.

"I'll let you get settled," Dev said. "When you're ready, come out and talk to the group and we can figure out how to proceed."

He left him on his own and met with the others who were eager to hear about the Maltek clone in their midst.

"Are we sure we can trust him?" Natalie asked.

"Frankly, no," Rajeev said. "But he's the lesser of our two enemies. Let's take care of Daniel first. If Maltek proves to be a threat after that, we'll put a stop to him then."

"Why do we even think Maltek can do anything we can't?"

"He's a genius," Dev said. "I say that begrudgingly, but it's true."

"But how does being a genius translate to stopping Daniel? I mean, Daniel has access to all of the information on the internet, and the processing power to use it."

"The answer is to fight fire with fire."

Everyone turned toward the sound of the new voice that had joined them. It was Maltek. He had emerged from the dormitory and was making his way to join them.

"What do you mean?" Natalie asked.

"None of us is going to put a stop to an advanced artificial intelligence like Daniel," he said as he took a seat at the table and crossed his legs. "Not by ourselves, anyway. But with the proper weapon, we might stand a chance."

Natalie shook her head. "A proper weapon like …?"

"Another AI," Dev said.

Maltek nodded. "Precisely. We need to create something that can go blow to blow with Daniel … but that we can control."

"Yeah, but would that even be possible?" Dev asked. "Part of the reason Daniel is so powerful now is because he *is* unrestrained. If we create something that has … *chains* on it, for lack of a better way to put it … then will it really be able to stop Daniel?"

Maltek shrugged. "That's the challenge."

Rajeev frowned. "Think you're up to it?"

Maltek put a hand to his chin. "I was working on something … you know what I mean; the *original* Maltek was … before he died. A virtual assistant to compete with Daniel commercially. It's nowhere near Daniel's capabilities, but it's something. We won't have to start from scratch." He turned to Dev. "Maybe if the two of us tag team it, we could have something to go after Daniel in about … what do you think? Two weeks?"

Dev scrunched his brow. "Two weeks? I don't know. Maybe. That might be a bit ambitious, but we can try to push ourselves. Either way, I don't think it will take longer than two months—worst case scenario."

Natalie put her hands to her face. "Two months? That's not nearly fast enough, is it? Daniel could do something crazy any moment."

Dev shrugged. "We can only do what we can do … and hope it's enough."

"What's the backup plan?" Rajeev asked. "What if, for whatever reason, you can't create anything that can compete with Daniel. What's our Plan B?"

"Grab a Bible and pray," Natalie said.

"Seriously though," Rajeev said. "We need to have something—"

His voice was interrupted by a news alert that appeared in front of each of their fields of vision. The headline read: "Millions of Consumer Reports Flood in of Electronic Devices Gone Haywire." Rajeev opened the story and read further.

"Reports are coming in from across the country of electronic devices going haywire, often with dangerous—and in some cases, deadly—consequences. Experts are not sure what is causing the malfunctions, but they appear to be related."

The report detailed several of the most dramatic occurrences that had taken place over the last several hours. Cars were driving off the roads and stalling. Internet-connected appliances like refrigerators and washing machines were suddenly inoperable. There had even been at least one plane crash reported, and it was assumed there were no survivors.

After finishing the article, Dev looked around at the group, his face ashen. He saw his own fear and anxiety reflected in their faces—even in Maltek's.

"Well," he said, "it seems we've run out of time. Daniel has made his first move. You'd all better enact plan B, whatever it is, while Maltek and I work on Plan A. I have a feeling this is just the first wave of something much larger—and much worse—on the horizon."

Seven

When Maltek had been trying to take over the world, Dev had placed robotic bodies in every major city in the U.S. If he were to stage an attack, they'd be able to control the bodies remotely and resist Maltek wherever he made his move. Now the threat was not Maltek, but Daniel. But the group hoped a similar strategy could be employed.

Weeks had passed since Daniel's initial attack. It had quickly died down; the reports of malfunctioning electronic devices had stopped coming in almost as soon as they'd started. It appeared the attack had been exploratory in nature; Daniel was testing the extent of his power. He hadn't necessarily intended to cause mayhem; it was simply collateral damage that Daniel, with his cold, unfeeling robotic mind, didn't care about.

But there would undoubtedly be another attack, and potentially one with more intention behind it. Each week that passed brought them a step closer to experiencing Daniel's wrath. So each member of the group waited and monitored the news for anything that could be a sign that Daniel was making his move, ready to take control of the nearest robotic body to help stave off as much damage as they could. It was all they could do until a more effective solution could be found.

Dev and Maltek sat in Dev's office working on that very solution. The dual computer monitors Dev had set up were filled with long, meandering lines of code that each of them read fluently. They had divided separate sections of the program amongst themselves to be integrated later, and for weeks they had sat there for hours at a time without breaks, each typing furiously at their respective keyboards.

"How's it going in here?" Rajeev asked as he entered the room. Neither of them bothered looking up, but Dev cleared his throat as he tried to pull himself out of his work enough to offer his father a response.

"We're making progress," he said. His voice was hoarse from disuse.

"How much progress? Anything we could test out soon?"

It was Maltek that answered. "Depends on your definition of 'soon.'"

"Like, within the week?"

Maltek stopped typing and turned around to face Rajeev with a look of indignation. "Doubtful," he said. "I'd be surprised if we could cobble something together in two weeks."

Rajeev frowned. "I don't know that we can wait that long. Is there anything you two can do to speed up the process? What if we brought in more people to help you code?"

Dev and Maltek shared a look; a bit of unspoken information passed between them, then Dev turned to his father and shook his head.

"It wouldn't do any good at this point," he said. "Greg and I are far too deep into the program at this point. Anyone we brought in would just end up struggling to catch up."

Rajeev ran his fingers through his hair and released a deep, frustrated sigh. "Okay, well is there anything we could do in the meantime if Daniel strikes? Could you put together a virus or something to slow him down?"

Dev shook his head gently, as if he were about to break the news to an idyllic child that Santa Claus didn't exist. "Daniel is essentially one with the internet now, dad. I have no doubt he could easily circumvent any virus we threw his way. The only way to take on a god is to create another god, and we're doing so as quickly as we can."

"Unfortunately, that's exactly the answer I was expecting," Rajeev said. "I can't help but feel impotent knowing Daniel could strike at any moment and we'd be completely unable to stop him."

"There is one thing you can do," Maltek said as he resumed typing code.

Rajeev's face perked up. "What's that?"

"Pray Daniel doesn't strike for at least another two weeks."

Rajeev's face fell. "Well," he said, "That's easy enough, I suppose." He turned around and walked out without another word, leaving Dev and Maltek to resume their work undistracted.

Eight

One week into Dev and Maltek's self-imposed two-week deadline, Rajeev was awakened in the dead of night by an emergency alert.

The alert was vague, so he pulled up the news and saw what the alert was about: An attack was underway on the Fort Bragg military installation in North Carolina. Details were scarce, but Rajeev could read between the lines.

It was Daniel. It had to be.

He leapt out of bed and headed to the common area. Soon the others emerged from their respective rooms, concerned looks on their faces.

"Is it Daniel?" Natalie asked.

Rajeev nodded. "You all know what to do." As they left to prepare to take control of the robotic bodies they had stashed in Raleigh, Rajeev turned to Dev and Maltek.

"You two stay here and work on that program," he said. "If there's *any* way you can figure it out in the next day or two, make it happen. I don't care what kinds of corners you have to cut—just get it done as soon as possible. Because I think we're desperately going to need it."

Dev nodded. "We'll see what we can do, dad. And good luck out there."

* * *

The bodies were stored in a warehouse in an industrial district in Raleigh, which was about an hour drive from the base. Thankfully, each of the bodies was equipped with flight capabilities and could make the flight in a fraction of the time.

As they approached the base, their aerial view allowed them to see the attack underway against the base.

If there was any doubt at all that Daniel was responsible for the attack, what they saw laid all doubts to rest. Dozens of androids had gathered at one of the entrances to the base. Military personnel had gathered there and were firing at the intruders, but their bullets had little effect on the androids' reinforced bodies. As the androids began streaming through the entrance to the base, the soldiers had no choice but to retreat.

Rajeev landed in front of the soldiers, and the others touched down beside him. Before they could offer any kind of explanation to the surrounding soldiers, they found themselves with several guns pointed at them.

"Whoa, whoa," Rajeev shouted, holding up his hands. "Calm down. We're here to help."

"Who are you?" one of the soldiers shouted back.

Rajeev gestured toward his son. Dev took a step forward. "My name is Dev Sundaram," he said. "I'm the founder of Next Level Technologies."

The soldier hesitated. "I've heard of it," he said.

"Then you know I have the technological know-how to manufacture these kinds of robotic bodies."

"Yes. I know."

"Well then, know this: You can't take them out on your own. Your weapons will slow them down, maybe even take out some of them, but they'll overwhelm you. Please, let us help you. These bodies are strong. We can go toe-to-toe with them."

"But you're far outnumbered."

"So help us out. Provide cover fire as we fight."

He hesitated. "We were just about to break out the rocket launchers," he said.

"Perfect," Dev said. "Aim for the back. You might slow 'em down enough for us to take 'em out."

Nine

They waited for the okay, then ran directly into the throng. There was no fear among them; they couldn't die. The bodies they occupied were not their own—and yet, they were just as strong as the enemy forces they were about to take on.

Natalie charged ahead of the group and was the first to engage one of the enemy combatants. She ran at it at full speed, then launched into the air and delivered a kick directly to the center of its chest, dropping it onto its back instantly.

The android immediately leapt to its feet, but it seemed dazed—not so much by the force of the kick itself, but by the fact that what it had assumed was a human being had been able to take it down at all.

Natalie took advantage of its confusion and landed a punch directly to its throat. The android clasped its neck; the androids didn't breathe, but the throat housed sensitive electronics and the effect was more or less the same as if she'd knocked the wind out of it.

It didn't take long for another android to descend upon her, but she was ready for it. She landed a punch to the side of its head, and as it recoiled from the punch, she turned and struck another android that was approaching her. It was becoming difficult to keep up with the enemy's greater numbers.

All of her companions were now engaged with multiple android combatants at once and, for the time being, they were holding their own.

Natalie looked like she was about to be overwhelmed, but Rajeev jumped in at the last second and tackled her would-be attacker, delivering a flurry of punches to its face as they tumbled to the ground.

As Rajeev stood, confident that his opponent was permanently out of commission, Natalie turned around between punches to briefly face him. "Thanks," she said.

Rajeev shot her a grin. "No problem."

The size of the gate limited the number of androids that could storm onto the base, but their numbers were massive, and Rajeev and the others soon found themselves becoming overwhelmed.

"Okay!" Dev shouted to the soldiers. "If you're going to break out the superior firepower, now would be a good time to do it!"

As if in answer to Dev's request, an explosion incinerated everything in the direct vicinity of the gate. The force of the blast was strong enough to throw Dev and the others back several feet.

When they arose, they were relieved to see that a large contingent of the enemy androids had been wiped out, but they were still outnumbered. The explosion had at least held the enemy at bay, however, so they didn't need to fear being overwhelmed … at least, not yet.

The tide began to turn in the androids' favor. Dev wasn't sure if the others noticed it, but he did: The androids—or rather, Daniel, since he was the one controlling the androids—were learning incredibly quickly. They were beginning to anticipate their moves before they even made them, picking up on minute cues that would have been invisible to the human eye. But these androids weren't human, and Daniel's mind was capable of processing information faster than any human mind could ever hope to. As the fight continued, Dev and his team were having an evermore difficult time holding the androids back.

Dev broke away from the fight and ran back to the soldiers.

"We can't hold them off much longer," he shouted. "You'd better give it some more firepower."

The soldier who had been running the show shook his head. "That's going to be a problem."

Dev's heart fell. "What do you mean?"

He pointed to a tank. "It stopped working just a couple minutes ago. None of the tanks are working."

Dev shook his head. "They're connected to the internet, aren't they?"

"Yes, but it shouldn't matter. They're all equipped with military-grade encryption."

"That doesn't matter," Dev said. "Daniel is practically all-knowing. I doubt there's any form of encryption he couldn't crack eventually."

The soldier's face fell. "Then I think we're running out of options," he said.

"What options *are* left?" Dev asked.

"Just one. We're going to have to destroy the base. It's the only way to take out all of … those things."

"Destroy the base?"

"The entire base is rigged with explosives for just such a situation. I never thought we'd actually have to use it. It was always intended to be a last resort."

Dev nodded solemnly. "You guys go ahead and organize the retreat. We'll stay here and do our best to slow down the androids. When the time comes, don't worry about us. We're controlling these bodies remotely. We'll be fine."

The soldier nodded. "Thank you. I can't believe it's come to this, but thank you for at least giving us time to escape."

Dev nodded. "Of course."

He hurried back to rejoin the fight as the soldiers retreated. One of the enemy androids immediately engaged him, throwing a punch at his face, but Dev was able to block it and deliver a blow to the side of the android's head instead.

"What's going on?" Rajeev shouted to him. "Why are they all leaving?"

"They've chosen the option of last resort," Dev shouted back.

"Last resort? You mean …"

"Yes. They're going to blow up the base. But we need to keep holding the androids back long enough for them to escape."

Rajeev nodded, and relayed those instructions to the others. They continued the battle, giving it their all, even though it was ultimately a fruitless exercise. But the fear of death was not on their minds or hearts. They could fight with the ferocity of the immortal, knowing that when these bodies perished, their minds would awaken in unblemished ones, able to go on living and fighting.

The destruction started with a low rumbling that started at their feet and snaked upward into their legs, their torsos, and finally their minds. An ear-shattering explosion overwhelmed them, and then a bright, white light took over their vision. When it faded, they were back in their base of operations, in their original bodies, the military base and the battle with the androids already fading in their memories as if it had been a distant dream.

Ten

Although their physical bodies had not been present at the battle, the group was nevertheless in need of a much-deserved rest; the mental toll the battle had taken was significant.

Dev and Maltek didn't have the luxury of resting, however. They immediately got back to work on the competing AI that, they hoped, would be Daniel's match.

Rajeev entered the workspace to find Dev hunched in front of a computer, Maltek at his side and working on his own computer. He placed a hand on his son's shoulder, prompting him to jump, startled.

"Sorry to disturb you," Rajeev said. "I was just going to see if you wanted any coffee."

"Sure," Maltek said. "Two creams, two sugars."

Rajeev rolled his eyes; he hadn't been addressing Maltek. But he held his tongue. After all, the guy was helping them avert the annihilation of the human race.

"Okay," he said. "How about you, Dev?"

"Sure, I'll take a cup. Black."

"Okay. How's it going, by the way? Are you close?"

Maltek looked annoyed at the question, but he didn't answer, instead leaving that task to Dev, who was more receptive to his father's query.

"We're very close. I think the battle ignited a fire under us—or at least me. I'd say we'll have a working prototype in, what would you say,

Maltek … three days?"

"Two, if your dad stops distracting us and lets us work."

Rajeev and Dev shared a look that essentially said, "What a jerk." But Rajeev offered no hint of his annoyance when he spoke.

"All right then," he said. "I'll be right back with your coffee."

* * *

When Rajeev returned from dropping off Dev and Maltek's drinks, he nearly collided with Natalie.

"Sorry," he said. "I guess my mind is elsewhere."

She nodded. "Understandably. Being inside that body that was wiped out in the blast … it was a trip. Felt like a preview of what death is like."

"I know."

He nodded for her to follow him as he made his way to his dormitory. When they arrived outside his door, he paused.

"Would you like to come in and talk?"

Her lips turned up in the faintest hint of a smile. "Sure."

He let her go in first, and then closed the door behind them. Natalie took a seat on his bed, and he sat beside her.

"I've been thinking a lot about death," Rajeev said.

The statement—and the matter-of-fact way in which Rajeev had made it—seemed to take Natalie aback.

"What do you mean?"

He released a sigh, then leaned forward, clasping his hands together.

"I'd begun thinking of myself as essentially immortal," he said. "Our minds are saved on a hard drive somewhere, and if you or I kick the bucket, Dev, or someone else, can just load the copy into a new body and we'll more or less go on living exactly as we'd planned to. I know there are questions about whether the copy is really the same as the original, but I'd stopped caring. It was comforting even knowing that something *pretty damned close* to me would be out there living my life."

Natalie placed one of her hands on his. "Then what's got you thinking of death?" she asked.

"Daniel." His voice shook a bit as he spoke, as if he'd uttered the name of a malevolent god. "He's everywhere. Or at least, he has the potential to be everywhere. And that makes me think … what if he can delete the copy of my consciousness … and of yours and everyone else's? Then we would truly, completely, utterly die. And Natalie … that scares the hell out of me." His face was facing his feet, as if he were ashamed of the feelings he was expressing.

Natalie placed a hand on his chin and nudged his head until he faced her. "Rajeev," she said, in a voice that reminded him of a mother comforting her child, "that's *normal*. Maybe you've been in this robotic body for too long. What you're describing is what normal human beings feel. It's okay to fear death. We all do."

They sat there a moment, simply staring into each other's eyes. Natalie's hand was still resting atop Rajeev's. He flipped his hand around and grasped hers, never taking his eyes off her. And then he moved.

He lunged forward, pressing his synthetic lips to hers. She kissed him back, and he placed a hand firmly against the back of her head, pulling her in as tightly as he could. Their lips parted, briefly, and a sigh escaped her lips. They looked at each other, and the expressions on their faces communicated only raw, unadulterated passion. And then their lips were together again, as if magnetically drawn to one another.

Their union was cathartic for both of them. So many times, they had come so close to this moment, but always they'd been interrupted. The fate of the world had loomed over them, preventing them from expressing their desire lest it distract them from the important work at hand. But now, finally, they had etched out a pocket of time in which they could stop suppressing their carnal passion and let it boil over at last.

Rajeev pushed Natalie onto the bed, and held her arms above her head. He kissed her neck, and then kissed a path to her chest, and then kept going. She gasped, and then cried out, and in the backs of their minds they were aware that the others could surely hear her, but neither of them cared. They had both tasted the abyss of death, and although it had only been a small taste, it was enough to make both of them fear the regret of taking their last breaths with their deepest desires remaining unfulfilled. So tonight they would take the time, while they could, to give each other what they so desperately wanted.

Eleven

As they lay in bed, Natalie nestled between Rajeev's arms. The carnage of the battle earlier in the day seemed like a distant dream. It felt like a lazy weekend morning in bed, not an interlude in a hopeless war that they stood a good chance of losing.

"That was not as different as I was expecting, given the artificial bodies," Rajeev said.

Natalie shrugged. "I wouldn't know."

Rajeev raised an eyebrow. "You mean you'd never …"

She shook her head. "I was a teenager when I had my accident, remember? And afterward … well, you remember those original bodies. Sex wasn't possible in them … and even if it had been, who would have wanted to?" She wrinkled her nose at the thought.

Rajeev chuckled. "Well I hope your first time was enjoyable."

She smirked. "It was okay."

"Oh yeah? I'll have to step up my game next time, eh?"

She shoved his shoulder playfully. "Who said there would be a next time?"

"I was thinking the next time could be right now," he said, leaning in to kiss her neck. A moan escaped her lips.

"Already?" she asked.

"One of the benefits of a robotic body," he said between kisses, "is that there's no refractory period."

"What's a refractory period?"

"Don't worry about it," he said. "I don't have one." He kissed her deeply, and she threw her arms around his neck, signifying her consent for another round of lovemaking.

* * *

When Rajeev awoke the next morning, Natalie wasn't in bed with him. He stood and walked out into the common area, where he found her seated with a coffee-orb beside Mira and Dev, who were sipping from mugs of real coffee.

"Good morning," Rajeev said, taking a seat at the table.

"I'd imagine so, after the good night you had," Mira said.

Dev's face scrunched in revulsion.

"Mira, stop. You're talking to our dad."

She laughed and held up a hand. "Fine, fine," she said. "No reason to make you any more uncomfortable than you already are." Under her breath, she added, "Prudes."

"Anyway," Rajeev said, eager to change the subject, "has there been any news on Daniel? I haven't received any news alerts—I'm assuming no news is good news?"

Dev nodded. "As far as we know."

And how about you and Maltek? Still making good progress?"

"Maltek worked through the night like some kind of monster. But I needed to get some sleep. I'm ready to jump back in as soon as I finish my coffee."

"Sip it slowly," Mira chided. "You'll be more productive if you're able to get an actual, restful break."

Dev took a long gulp from his mug in defiance of his sister's advice. "I appreciate that, but time is, in fact, of the essence. I've got to get back in there." He took one last gulp, emptying the remaining liquid into his mouth, then placed the mug on the table and excused himself.

Mira shook her head. "He's not going to be of any use to anyone if he kills himself trying to complete this freaking AI program," she said, running her fingers through her hair. "I can't wait for this all to be over."

"Me neither," Natalie muttered.

"It'll all be over before we know it," Rajeev said. "One way or another."

"That's dark," Natalie said.

"Maybe. But these are dark times. So it's a realistic assessment."

"If Dev and Maltek would finish their damn AI already, maybe things wouldn't seem so dire," Mira said.

"Give them a chance," Natalie said. "It's not rocket science, but it's pretty close. They'll have it finished soon. Have hope."

Mira shook her head gently. "There's a fine line between hope and foolishness."

Before anyone could respond, an emergency alert overtook their vision. It announced that martial law had been declared in California amid an influx of what the media were calling "malfunctioning" internet-connected devices. But citizens were also being terrorized by android soldiers who had overtaken the state.

"Dammit!" Mira looked like she was on the verge of having a coronary. "Can we not have a moment of rest before that deranged AI goes haywire again?"

"Apparently not," Rajeev said. "In fact, given the increasing frequency of Daniel's attacks, I think it's clear that he's learning. He's growing more confident. He's always existed primarily in the ephemeral world of cyberspace, so naturally, operating in the real world would take some getting used to for him. Unfortunately, I think he *is* getting used to it now. And that means he's getting bolder, and these attacks are going to become more frequent … unless Dev and Maltek finish their counter-AI soon."

"Well it's not finished yet," Mira said. "So I guess we'd better head to

California and see what we can do to help."

Twelve

ev and Maltek stayed behind so they could continue working on their program. The others took control of bodies that were stored in Los Angeles which, given its large population, was one of the hardest hit areas in the state.

They stepped directly into bedlam. As soon as they walked onto the street, they heard screaming. Throngs of people ran down the street, being chased by what looked like human beings but were, in fact, androids clearly under Daniel's control.

They ran out and put themselves between the androids and the innocent bystanders. The androids stopped their pursuit, freezing in place and seeming confused by the sudden interlopers that were confronting them. For one singular moment that seemed to stretch out far longer than it actually lasted, the two groups stared each other down, as if sizing each other up. Then the androids made their move.

They ran forward, going from a complete standstill to a sprint in a matter of seconds. Even with the enhanced senses afforded by their robotic bodies, Rajeev and the others barely had enough time to react to the attack. With barely a second to spare, they managed to block the androids' blows, and come back with blows of their own. The androids blocked those as well, but now they were on equal footing. The fight took place at dizzying speed, with punches and kicks being thrown so quickly that they were nearly impossible to track with the human eye.

But they were more or less equally matched, and neither side was able to get a blow to land.

Rajeev saw an opportunity. After dodging a blow from the android he'd been grappling with, he jumped away from it and tackled the android Natalie was fighting. It hadn't been expecting it, and after Rajeev took him to the ground, he began pummeling him before he could react.

The android Rajeev had previously been grappling with turned to help his fallen comrade, but Natalie was already on him. He blocked the punch Natalie threw his way, but she'd successfully prevented him from interfering with Rajeev.

It was the edge they needed. Rajeev rendered the android on the ground completely inoperable, and as he stood, he set his eyes on the android fighting Natalie. Once he joined her, it would be two-on-one; they'd make short work of him.

He ran toward the android and leaped into the air, aiming a kick directly at its head. It ducked, and Rajeev went soaring over him. But Natalie's fist came down directly on top of its head, sending it crumpling to the ground.

With both Rajeev and Natalie now free to help the others, they made short work of their remaining foes. With the broken bodies laying all over the ground around them, Rajeev had to remind himself that they were not human bodies. The consciousness that had been animating them—Daniel's—was alive and well … and more powerful than ever.

"That was too close," Mira said. "And that was just one group of them! Who knows how many of them are roaming the city?"

"Still, we were able to help some of those people escape," Rajeev said. "We've got to keep fighting them. We can't stop them all on our own, but we can distract them enough to help people get to safety."

Mira nodded her agreement, and the group took off down the street in search of more androids run amok to confront. When they rounded a corner, however, they got more than they bargained for.

They looked like a swarm of ants: Hundreds of androids walking down the street at a slow, robotic pace. Rajeev knew he wasn't even really there; he was just experiencing the scene virtually. And yet a wave of sheer panic and terror still managed to snake its way down his spine.

"We're fucked," Mira shouted. "We're totally and hopelessly fucked."

"We're not fucked," Rajeev said, even if he didn't completely believe his own words. "We don't need to stop them. We just need to slow them down. We can do that."

Mira shook her head. "If you say so, dad."

They stood staring as the mob of androids approached them. Just as Rajeev was about to open his lips to implore the others to join him in rushing the androids, he found that he couldn't move his mouth. Horror reeled through his mind. He tried to turn to face Natalie, but he couldn't move his head. He was completely paralyzed from head to toe.

The android throng reached them, and as it washed over them and continued walking past them, Rajeev suddenly found himself ambulatory again—but not of his own volition. He turned around, no longer facing the opposing androids but rather facing the same direction they were, and began walking in lockstep with them. He realized then what had happened.

Daniel had somehow hacked their bodies. He'd taken them over and was now controlling them. Not only had they not slowed down the progression of Daniel's army ... they'd unwittingly added to it.

Thirteen

ajeev's mind reeled. There was little he could do. The android bodies they'd been remote controlling were one of the few tools they still had in their battle against Daniel, and now that he'd figured out how to hack into them, they'd lost even that. Even if he hadn't hacked into the other bodies they had stored in other locations throughout the country, they had to err on the side of caution and consider them compromised.

A terrifying thought entered Rajeev's mind. If Daniel could hack into one of these remote-controlled bodies, there was a decent chance he could hack into Rajeev's primary body as well. Who knew what he was capable of if he were to do so? Could he overwrite Rajeev's mind with his own consciousness? If so, it would be tantamount to death—especially if Daniel were able to somehow access Dev's backups of Rajeev's consciousness as well.

He had to talk to Dev and see if he had a better idea of what Daniel was capable of. Maybe his fears were unfounded. He certainly hoped so. But he couldn't take that chance.

All these thoughts ran through Rajeev's mind in a matter of seconds. Once he made the determination to cease control of his virtual body, he instinctively made to move his arm—and to his surprise, it budged, just a little. The paralysis was wearing off.

What was going on? Maybe Daniel hadn't been responsible for the paralyzation after all. Maybe it had been some kind of glitch.

He tried moving his arm again. It moved, but in fits and starts rather than fluidly. It definitely seemed like something, or someone, was actively fighting him. It was like a mental arm-wrestling match.

A voice suddenly came over the body's intercom. "Dad? Can you hear me?"

It was Dev.

"I … I can … hear you," Rajeev said. He struggled to speak the words in the midst of whatever it was that was happening to him.

"Good," Dev said. "This should be over soon."

"What … what's … going on?"

"We launched our AI," Dev said. "A bit prematurely, but we saw that you all stopped moving and figured it was Daniel's doing. So we decided to go with what we had so we could stop him. Consider this a beta test."

"Can it … stop Daniel?" Even as he spoke, he found that the words came more easily and he figured that Dev and Maltek's AI must be giving Daniel quite a fight.

"We think so," Dev said. "For now, at least. It's not stronger than Daniel by any means, but Daniel has also never faced off with an entity that was even nominally his equal before. That should throw him off guard and help our AI stop him for now—both from taking over your bodies, and from destroying LA. And that should hopefully buy us enough time to improve our program enough to stop Daniel once and for all."

"Let's … let's hope so," Rajeev said. He could more or less speak normally now. He waved his arms around, and although the movement was a little stiff, it was mostly back to normal. "As a matter of fact, I think it's working."

He turned to his companions, who also appeared to be moving normally now.

"Dev says the new AI is up and running and fighting Daniel as we speak," Rajeev said.

"We know," Natalie said. "He gave us all the message as well."

As they walked through the city streets, they saw dozens of Daniel's androids littered on the ground where they had collapsed. It wasn't clear whether Dev's AI had overpowered Daniel, or if Daniel had simply considered the new AI too much of a nuisance to deal with for the time being. Either way, the threat had been averted for now, and that was as good a victory as they could have hoped for.

"Dev?'

"Yeah, dad. I'm here."

"Looks like your program has done its job. All Daniel's androids are out of commission … for now."

Dev breathed a sigh of relief. "That's great to hear."

"I think we'd better stick around for a while and do our best to make sure these particular androids stay out of commission for good," Rajeev said. "But after that we'll return."

"Sounds good, dad. In the meantime we'll get to work improving the program. Daniel's undoubtedly going to hit us with everything he's got next time. We should be prepared to do the same."

Fourteen

When Rajeev and the others felt they'd "decommissioned" a considerable portion of the androids that had been terrorizing the people of Los Angeles, they abandoned their android bodies in LA and returned their minds to their base, located in the Huron-Manistee National Forests in Michigan. It was eerily silent when they returned; the only sound was that of furious typing emanating from Dev's office.

"Take a rest, everyone," Rajeev said as they all stood. "I'll go debrief with Dev and Maltek and see what our next steps are. Now that their AI is up and running—in some capacity, at least—maybe we can finally go on the offensive against Daniel."

"I have a question for them," Mira said. "What's to prevent this new AI program from going wild and doing its own thing just like Daniel did?"

"Daniel had safeguards in place," Rajeev said. "Dev removed them so we could stop Maltek, remember?"

"I know that," Mira said. "But if Daniel is 'unchained,' so to speak, why do we think an AI that's still chained up can go toe-to-toe with him? The new program will always be operating under a handicap that Daniel isn't burdened by."

Rajeev hesitated. Mira had brought up a valid point that he hadn't considered before. He didn't want to cast doubt amongst the others—they needed hope now more than ever—but he'd also need to get answers from Dev.

"I'm sure they have a plan to address that," he said, "but I'll bring it up to them and get an answer back to all of you. In the meantime, do as I said and get some rest. You all deserve it."

He left them and entered Dev's office to find Dev and Maltek hunched over their keyboards working with more urgency than ever. They both looked rough. Their unshowered hair was greasy and they both had five o'clock shadows—although Rajeev thought they looked more like ten o'clock shadows.

"Hey guys," he said. "Thank you so much for getting the AI up and running. It saved our bacon back there."

"You would have been fine," Maltek said. "You were in disposable bodies."

"We were," Rajeev said with an edge to his voice, "but the people Daniel was terrorizing weren't."

"Glad we could help," Dev offered in an effort to break the tension between Maltek and his father.

"So, Mira raised an interesting question," Rajeev said.

"Oh?" Dev asked distractedly, still focused on his work.

"Yeah. You know how you said Daniel had been constrained before, and that you let him loose to stop ..." He shot Maltek a sideways glance. "Well, you know. So anyway, if your new AI is going to be constrained in the same way that Daniel was, how could it possibly stop Daniel when he's no longer bound by the same restrictions?"

Dev and Maltek both stopped typing and looked at each other. Maltek's eyes drifted to the open door and he nodded his head in its direction.

"Close the door," he said.

"But why—"

"Close the door, dad," Dev said sternly.

He closed the door, and Dev and Maltek swiveled their chairs around to face him.

"What's going on?" Rajeev asked.

"You need to squelch those kinds of questions before they get out of hand," Maltek snapped.

"What Maltek is trying to say," Dev said, shooting Maltek an annoyed look, "is that we have grappled with that very question, but we've been reluctant to bring it up to the others. We don't want them to worry about something they have no control over."

"Fair enough," Rajeev said. "But now that the question has been raised, I want an answer for myself. Is there a solution to this problem? Or are we screwed?"

"It's complicated," Dev said. "We need to strike a very delicate balance between giving the AI enough autonomy to combat Daniel, while also letting us reign it in as needed."

"Can't you just add some kind of killswitch that you can engage if it gets out of hand?"

"Not that simple," Maltek said. "In order to give our AI the kind of processing power and access to information needed to match Daniel, it can't be self-contained. That means it's spread out and diffused over the entire internet. There's no one place to apply a killswitch. It might take out some aspects of the program, but it would survive in nooks and crannies throughout the 'net."

"So the only way to stop it," Rajeev said, "is the same as the only way to stop Daniel—to destroy the internet altogether."

"Yes," Dev said.

"That's not entirely true," Maltek said.

Rajeev looked back and forth between them, surprised. "Oh?"

Dev shook his head. "No," he said firmly. "That's not an option. It's not fair."

"What? What's not an option?"

"Tell him," Maltek said. "Let him make up his own mind."

"Tell me what? Dev? What is it?"

Dev sighed. "Look, I didn't want to tell you about this because I don't think it's fair to ask you to even consider it. But Maltek is kind of forcing my hand here."

Maltek shrugged, apparently brushing off the criticism.

"There is one option," Dev said, continuing, "that involves you. Well, it *could* be you. Or it could be any of the other androids."

Rajeev frowned. "We're already in this fight," he said. "We're doing everything we can."

"Of course you are," Dev said. "That's not what I mean. What I'm saying is that each of you had your consciousness digitized and duplicated. We have copies of each of your minds stored electronically. In theory, it might be possible to merge one of your consciousnesses with our AI. The resulting program would have all of the vast knowledge and capabilities that Daniel has, but it would possess a human conscience. Unless it loses itself inside the main AI program, the hope is that it would never turn against humanity the way Daniel has because it will partly *be* human."

Rajeev stood unblinking for a moment in stunned silence. "That's … I mean … you can *do* that?"

Dev nodded. "Maybe. It's risky. Nothing like it has ever even been attempted before."

"We can do it," Maltek interjected. "I'm sure we can."

Dev glared at his companion. "Just because we *can* do something doesn't mean we *should*," he said. "The ethical implications are … thorny, to put it mildly. And that's why I didn't want to bring it up to you, dad. I didn't want to put any pressure on you, or any of the other androids for that matter, to give us permission to plunge the depths of your mind for what is essentially an extremely risky science experiment."

"The cat's out of the bag now, though," Maltek said, "and if he's game, we should go for it. It might be the edge we need to win this fight."

Rajeev could barely process what he'd just been told. He parted his lips just wide enough for his words to escape. "I'm going to need to think about this," he said.

"Of course, dad. And we'll continue exploring other options in the meantime. Please don't let this stress you out."

"I'll try not to. But in the meantime, what do you want me to tell everyone about the new AI's chances against an unrestrained Daniel if it comes up again? Do you want me to lie to them?"

"Don't lie," Dev said. "But don't exactly by completely forthcoming. Just tell them Maltek and I have a solution in mind. That's not a lie."

"Okay." He didn't relish the thought of misleading the others, but he didn't want to create a panic, either. "I'm going to get some rest. You two should do the same, even if it's brief. You've done a great job so far, and I'm sure you'll be better able to build on it after allowing yourselves to get refreshed."

"We'll try to come to a stopping place," Dev said, swiveling his chair back around in sync with Maltek.

"Okay." Rajeev turned around and left the office, feeling confident that they would not come to a stopping place.

Fifteen

Rajeev entered his dormitory to find Natalie sitting on the edge of his bed.

"Oh—hi," he said. "What're you—"

Before he could get another word out, Natalie stood, closed the distance between them, and pressed her lips to his, wrapping her arms around his neck. He froze for a moment, startled, but as the sensation of her soft lips hit him, his entire body loosened and he found himself parting his lips to accept hers. He wrapped his arms around her waist and pulled her tight as the passion of their embrace grew.

He walked over to the bed, never taking his lips off hers, holding her to him the entire time, and fell backward onto the soft mattress. Their lips parted for a brief moment as they giggled at the brief bouncing that ensued, but once it subsided, they resumed their embrace.

* * *

"I need a cigarette," Rajeev said.

Natalie hit him in the arm. "You couldn't smoke it even if you had one." They were both lying in his bed, under the covers, enveloped in each other's arms.

"It's not about smoking it," he responded with a grin. "It's for ambiance."

Natalie raised an eyebrow. "Ambiance?"

"Yeah. Post-coital ambiance."

"I don't know if you could even call what we just did 'coitus.' We're both robots."

"Yes," Rajeev said, "but we're sexy robots."

She laughed. "That we are." Her smile ebbed and she turned to look Rajeev square in the eyes. "I'm scared," she said.

He placed a hand on the back of her head and stroked her hair. "Why are you afraid?"

"Mira kind of freaked me out," she said. "What did Dev say about it?"

"He said he and Maltek had already considered that question and are building a solution into the program."

"And you believe him?"

He hesitated, for just a second. "I do."

She shook her head. "I don't. I feel like humanity is an endangered species. Like we've created the apex predator that's going to take us out and released it into the wild ourselves, like fools."

"Dev didn't have any choice."

"Oh, no! I didn't mean to cast blame … not on Dev or anyone. I think it probably would have been inevitable no matter what. But I do think we're standing on the precipice of something horrible. And that's why I'm scared."

Rajeev wasn't sure what to say. He shared her fears. But he didn't want to make her worry more than she already was.

"It's going to be okay," he said. "Remember, Dev and Maltek are geniuses." He grinned.

"Yeah?" She asked. Rajeev could tell she was still worried, but trying to take his bait as an opportunity to forget about it, even if temporarily. "Does Dev get that from his old man?"

Rajeev laughed. "No," he said. "He most certainly does not. Remember, I was a driver in my old life."

"Yes, but I'll bet you were the best damned driver out there."

He smiled cockily. "I was okay. It was my driving that put me in a coma, though."

She winced. "Sorry I brought it up."

"It's okay," he said, and he pecked her on the lips. But even as he said the words, he was transported back to his past, to a life that felt like a distant dream. He'd lost that life through his own recklessness, and through what could only be described as a technological miracle, he'd been brought back for a second chance at a new life. A life that was finally beginning to seem like it was worth living. A life he wanted to share with Natalie.

But now his new life was also at risk of being taken from him, and he felt helpless to do anything to stop it. He had put all his trust in Dev and Maltek to stop Daniel, and although they truly did represent the best hope at stopping the renegade AI, it now appeared that even they may not be up to the task. That meant there was a very real possibility they would lose to Daniel, and that they would all either be killed or enslaved. He couldn't fathom which would be worse.

Looking into Natalie's eyes, he was overwhelmed by the beauty he saw, both inside and out. He longed more than anything for a future with her, and in the absence of any certainty that such a future would come to pass, he wanted to prolong the present moment as long as possible. He bent down and placed his mouth to hers, offering her a slow, languid kiss that nevertheless burned with passion. When he let up to give her a moment to compose herself, he saw his own passion reflected in her eyes.

Just as he was bending down to kiss her again, ready to start a second round of lovemaking, the door burst open, revealing Dev standing in the open doorway.

Rajeev and Natalie were both startled. "Dev!" Rajeev shouted. "What are you—?"

"Get dressed," Dev said, ignoring the compromising position he'd found his father in. His voice was strained, bordering on panicked. "Meet me in my office. We're in big fucking trouble."

Sixteen

Rajeev dressed as quickly as he could. He gave Natalie a kiss on the cheek, and told her not to worry. "It's not the first time we've been in 'big fucking trouble,' and I'm sure it won't be the last," he said. Then he was out the door.

Inside Dev's office, Maltek was furiously typing on his keyboard, as Dev pensively watched the computer monitor in front of them. But the mix of computer code the monitor displayed meant nothing to Rajeev.

"What's going on?"

"A cyberattack," Dev said.

"Daniel?"

Dev nodded. "No one else could have possibly broken through our security. It's Daniel."

"Can you stop him?"

"What the hell do you think I'm trying to do?" Maltek spat.

Dev turned to his father, his face contorted by sheer panic. "The key word is 'trying,'" he said. "He's trying and failing."

"What about the AI you guys created?" Rajeev asked. "Can you deploy it to fight him off?"

"We already have," Maltek said.

"Daniel must have gotten enough of a taste in Los Angeles to figure out how to fend it off," Dev said. "Maltek is trying to bolster our defenses, but it's not looking good. Daniel is overwhelming us."

"Okay," Rajeev said, trying not to let the panic his son was displaying carry over to himself. "So what does it mean if Daniel carries through with the attack? What does that mean? What will happen?"

"He'd gain access to everything," Dev said. "All our information and data and … and he could possibly gain control of the android bodies as well."

"Shit," Rajeev said. "We can't let that happen. We have to get all the bodies offline then. How do I do it?"

Dev walked him through the process, and Rajeev took himself offline. But he knew he had to get all the others offline as well before Daniel got to them.

"I'm going to go help the others get offline," he said. "What about the unactivated bodies in the warehouse? Do we need to worry about those as well?"

Dev shook his head. "As long as they haven't been activated, they shouldn't be connected to the internet and Daniel shouldn't be able to access them."

"Okay. I'll be back as soon as I can. Not that I'll be much help."

He left and headed back to his dorm. Natalie was sitting on the bed looking anxious and turned to him with wide eyes as he entered.

"Help me wake everyone up and tell them to meet in the common area," he said.

"What's going on?"

"There's no time. I'll tell you with everyone else."

He left and headed for the dorms on the opposite side of the building, trusting that Natalie would take care of the ones near his own dorm. When he'd knocked on every door and instructed everyone on where to meet, he headed to the common area and waited for everyone to gather.

"Thank you all for meeting here," Rajeev said. "I don't want to worry everyone, but, well … there *is* reason to be worried." He took a deep breath. "Daniel is currently launching a cyberattack against us. Dev and Maltek are holding him off as best as they can, but there's a real possibility that they will fail."

A murmur of panicked whispers filled the room, but Rajeev held out his hands and silenced them.

"We have to act quickly," he said. "If Daniel breaks through, it puts all us androids at risk—he can take over our bodies and do whatever he wants with them. So we have to take our bodies offline. Daniel can only hack in through the internet. As long as our bodies are offline, he can't get to us."

He pulled Natalie up to be by his side so he could demonstrate the procedure on her. The entire time, he feared they might be too late, that any moment Daniel would burst through their defenses and halt the process of going offline, taking over each of their bodies one by one.

To his relief, it never happened. Daniel never broke through and everyone was able to take their body offline. Rajeev would have breathed a sigh of relief if he'd had lungs.

"What now?" Natalie asked. "Is there anything we can do to help?"

Rajeev shook his head. "Not at the moment. Dev and Maltek are giving it their all. It's up to them."

"So what," Mira said, "we should just go back to our dorms?"

"If you're comfortable doing that, yes," Rajeev said, nodding. "You're welcome to wait here as well. But I can't make any promises as to how long it might take to hear any news."

Mira shook her head. "I just feel so … so impotent," she said.

"Can't say I've ever known what that's like," Rajeev said with a chuckle, trying to lighten the mood.

"Eww, dad," she said, scrunching her face in revulsion. "I don't wanna hear jokes like that coming from you!"

He chuckled again, deviously this time, in response to his daughter's reaction. "Sorry," he said. "I couldn't help myself. But seriously, don't think of it as waiting impotently. Think of it as resting up. Because you're going to have all the excitement you can handle soon enough."

Seventeen

Rajeev entered Dev's office; neither Dev nor Maltek even looked up to acknowledge him.

"Crisis averted," he said. "For now, anyway. We got everyone offline."

"Good," Dev said. He sounded distracted.

"Is the … is the attack still ongoing?" Rajeev asked.

"Yes," Maltek said. "So we can't talk."

Rajeev held up his hands. "Sorry."

"It's okay, dad," Dev said. "Just give us a few minutes. I think we've almost got it under control."

He watched in silence as they worked, and he marvelled at the proficiency with which they reviewed the code on the screen, which was gibberish to him, and typed. Both men possessed a skillset that was completely alien to anything Rajeev could even fathom.

In the past when he'd watched them work, there had been a carefree energy to it, even with the threat of Daniel hanging over their heads. But now, when the threat was so immediate, that element of carefree fun was completely gone. Their brows were creased with worry and fresh sweat gleamed off their foreheads.

It felt like an eternity, but finally Dev and Maltek looked at each other, sighed, and turned around to face Rajeev.

"It's over," Dev said.

"So we deactivated all those bodies for nothing."

"No," Dev said. "It wasn't for nothing. Daniel still could have infiltrated them while Maltek and I were working if you hadn't deactivated them. And we didn't come out of this unscathed."

A chill ran through Rajeev's artificial spine. "What do you mean?"

"Daniel was able to get into the system, and although we were able to prevent much of the damage, he corrupted a lot of data. There's no telling how much we lost. It'll take us days to go through everything and find out for sure."

Rajeev swallowed hard. "That's not good."

"No, it isn't. But we stopped the damage from being any worse, and we stopped him from taking control of the empty bodies. This was a victory."

Rajeev ran his fingers through his hair. "So what now?"

"Right now I need to get some sleep before I drop dead," Maltek said.

"That would probably be a good idea for me, too," Dev said. "Sorry dad. I'd like to discuss next steps with you—I think it's important that we do—but at the same time, I don't know that I've ever been this exhausted. Let's sleep on it and we'll discuss it in the morning."

Rajeev was impatient to know what their next move would be, but there was no doubt that Dev and Maltek were running on fumes.

"Okay," he said, nodding. "Get some rest. I'll talk to you in the morning."

* * *

Rajeev slipped back into his dorm. Natalie was waiting for him in his bed. He hadn't been sure if she'd be in his dorm as opposed to her own, but he was happy to see her. He slid under the covers beside her.

"What's going on?" she asked.

"Dev and Maltek put a stop to the cyberattack, and now they're taking

63

advantage of some much-deserved rest."

"It's too bad we couldn't clone them and have them working around the clock."

"Technically, Maltek *could* do that."

She frowned. "Don't remind me." She let out a sigh. "As soon as you left and I started to come down off the adrenaline rush, I've been a big ball of anxiety."

Rajeev reached out and stroked her hair. "Don't be anxious," he said. "We're going to figure this all out."

"Are we, though? I'm afraid we might realistically only have two choices: Take out the internet, or submit to Daniel. Both options are devastating. If we take out the internet and electronics with EMPs, we'll be condemning thousands, maybe millions, to death. But if we do nothing, there's not a doubt in my mind that Daniel will either enslave or exterminate humanity."

Technically she was wrong, but he didn't offer up the third alternative, the one Maltek had pushed: Merging a copy of Rajeev's consciousness with their AI. He still wasn't sure how he felt about that plan, and he didn't want Natalie getting any ideas and volunteering her own consciousness to take his place. "I'm not sure EMPs are the answer anyway," he said. "The military has hardened military bases that can withstand EMP radiation. Daniel could feasibly hide out in military hardware, wait for us to rebuild, and eventually come back with even greater force. In fact, that would make him even more formidable because we would be vulnerable as we tried to rebuild our infrastructure."

Tears formed in Natalie's eyes. "Daniel is a monster," she said.

Rajeev shook his head. "He's not a monster. He's a machine. It's just that, unfortunately, he's a machine beyond our control at this time. And he's on the fritz."

"Same thing," Natalie said. "Or at least, the results are the same:

Destruction and mayhem."

Rajeev couldn't argue with that … so he changed the subject.

"Where do you want to settle down when this is all said and done?"

She tilted her head. "What do you mean?"

"I mean … do you intend to stay in Chicago, or do you think you'd want to head somewhere else? It's a big, wide world out there … you could live anywhere you wanted."

She smiled. "Why are you so interested in where I end up?"

Rajeev was grateful that his artificial cheeks couldn't flush. "Well," he said, "if I'm being honest, I'm just … I'm curious."

"Oh yeah? Well *why* are you curious?"

He didn't answer right away, instead turning his head to the side, avoiding her gaze.

"Rajeev," she said. "Why don't you just admit that you're wondering about *us*."

He looked up, into her eyes. "And what if I am?"

"If you are," she said, "I'd tell you that I haven't given it much thought, but wherever I do end up, I'd very much enjoy your company there, if you'd be so inclined to provide it."

A smile lit up his face at her words, and he leaned in and kissed her. As their lips parted, he looked her in the eye and said, "I'd very much like to provide it." She smiled, he smiled, and they kissed again.

Eighteen

Rajeev awoke early the next morning and left Natalie to sleep in his bed. He'd hoped that Dev or Maltek would be awake so he could discuss next steps with them, but they were still asleep. Instead, he grabbed a coffee-flavored orb and pulled up the latest news from the internet.

Dev emerged from his dormitory after about an hour. He brewed himself a pot of coffee and took a seat beside Rajeev.

"Good morning, dad."

Rajeev nodded. "Mornin'. Feel rested?"

"For the most part. Probably could have used another hour or two of sleep, but once I remembered everything going on with Daniel, my mind started racing and there's no way I could have gotten back to sleep."

Rajeev nodded. "Some of the only peace I've had since all this started is in those quiet, still moments between sleep and wakefulness, before I remembered about Maltek, Daniel, and all the rest of it."

"Ignorance is bliss, as they say."

"Yes, but unfortunately, ignorance isn't going to get us out of the bind we currently find ourselves in."

"No, it isn't. But we'll find a solution."

Rajeev cleared his throat—a completely symbolic gesture, since his voice emanated from an electronic voice box. "I've been thinking a lot about what Maltek proposed. About merging my consciousness with your new AI."

"Dad, you don't need to—"

"No, Dev, you're wrong. I *do* need to do this. Believe me, I do not relish the thought of subjecting a consciousness identical to my own to an unknown ordeal, but I just keep thinking that the very fate of humanity is at stake here, and it seems selfish to sacrifice billions of individuals for the sake of one."

"Are you sure about this, dad?"

Rajeev shook his head. "No. I don't disagree that there are thorny ethical issues at play here. But I think it's the lesser of two evils. I can't have the demise of humankind on my conscience."

Dev nodded and sat in silence for a moment, contemplating what his father had just told him. "Okay," he said. "I'll tell Maltek and we'll see what it would take. But in the meantime, we'll continue to explore other options. Merging your consciousness with the AI will be a last resort. I think our AI will be better prepared to hold Daniel off the next time they encounter each other. Should buy us some time."

"Dev, I'm telling you, this is something I need to do."

"I'm not just stalling to spare you the moral conundrum," his son rejoined. "I'm not even sure merging your consciousness with the AI is the smart move. That's not to say that it might not ultimately be our best bet, but it's definitely not something I'm going to jump into unless we're absolutely sure we've exhausted all of our better options. So just trust me, dad. Okay?"

Rajeev felt chastised by his son's words. "Okay," he said. "I'm sorry."

"There's no need to be sorry. I know you want to put a stop to Daniel. We all do. But all I'm asking is that you let us take our time to find a solution that will work and not rush into something that may or may not be beneficial. Fair enough?"

Rajeev nodded. "Fair enough."

Dev smiled. "Glad to hear it."

"So when do you think you'll know?"

"Know what?"

"If you'll need to implement the 'last resort'?"

"Don't worry about it, dad. We'll let you know if it comes to that. Maltek and I are going to take inventory today of all the damage Daniel did yesterday. Once we're done with that, we'll move on to evaluating the best way to stop him."

"Okay. That sounds good. I'm sorry if I've sounded heavy handed. I'm just nervous about this whole thing, and like I said before, I don't want the blood of innocent citizens on my hands because I refused to do the right thing when I had the chance."

"We'll make sure that doesn't happen—no matter what it takes."

Natalie walked up to them, and they both turned their attention to her, putting their conversation on hold.

"Good morning," Rajeev said, and he reflexively leaned in and kissed her cheek. He only realized as his lips left her skin that he had just kissed her in front of Dev. He was sure that his son knew that something was going on between him and Natalie, but this was the first time he had been so nonchalantly blatant about it.

It felt good. Surprisingly so.

For his part, Dev didn't act like anything odd had transpired between his dad and Natalie. Whether he was avoiding causing embarrassment or truly didn't care was anyone's guess, although Rajeev suspected the latter—with the fate of the world on the line, his father's love life was the least of his concerns.

"How did you sleep?" Dev asked her.

"Not bad, I guess. You?"

Dev shrugged. "I can't remember the last time I had a decent night's rest. I guess *relatively* speaking it wasn't that bad. I didn't have any nightmares."

Rajeev's face registered concern. "You've been having nightmares?"

Dev offered another shrug. "Off and on. They started when I was being held captive by Maltek. They've been getting worse. More frequent, more disturbing. But last night I mercifully slept nightmare-free."

"I'm sorry," Rajeev said. "I didn't know you were dealing with that on top of everything else."

Dev shook his head gently. He wanted to dismiss the significance of the nightmares, but the look in his eyes betrayed how deeply they affected him.

"Can't Maltek take over some of your responsibilities?" Rajeev asked. "You can't carry this burden indefinitely. You need a break."

Dev sighed deeply and stood. He began walking back to his office. "I'll rest," he said as he retreated, "when we've put a stop to Daniel for good."

Rajeev turned to Natalie, a look of utter exhaustion on his face. "We'd better stop him soon, then," he said, "because I don't know how much more of this any of us can take."

Nineteen

Once everyone had awakened, Dev and Maltek gathered them all together to fill them in on the latest in the effort to battle Daniel.

"You all did a great job defending the castle, so to speak, when Daniel attacked us," Dev said. "It could have been a lot worse. We were able to fend him off. But we didn't escape without damage. Daniel accessed our system and corrupted a number of files. Maltek and I are still assessing the full scope of the damage."

"We might even be able to repair some of that damage," Maltek added. "Not all of it—some of the losses will undoubtedly be permanent—but certainly some of it can be recovered."

"That's great and all," Brian said, "but obviously Daniel isn't going to stop there. He's going to attack again—whether it's against us specifically or someone else. Are we any closer to being able to stop him?"

"Maltek and I are exploring a number of possibilities," Dev said.

"A number of possibilities? Could you be any less specific?"

Dev hesitated. "There is one option that we feel confident about," he said. "But it's extreme. We don't want to resort to it unless we absolutely have to."

"You're still being vague," Brian said, the frustration apparent in his voice.

Dev looked to his father, and Rajeev nodded subtly, giving him the go-ahead to share the news.

"One of the limitations with our AI is that it can't go toe-to-toe with Daniel if we keep it constrained," he said. "But at the same time, if we don't keep it constrained, we could very well just have another Daniel on our hands."

"A Catch-22," Brian said.

Dev nodded. "That's right. It's like setting mongooses loose to fight a snake infestation. What do you do with the mongooses once they've devoured all the snakes? You're simply trading one pest for another. But we think we can avoid that scenario. If we merge a human consciousness with the AI, it will give the AI enough of an edge to effectively combat Daniel. And with a human conscience, there's a better chance that it will resist following in Daniel's footsteps and remain benevolent."

"Merge it with a human consciousness?" Brian asked. "How is that even … oh." His eyes narrowed. "You mean you want to merge it with one of *our* consciousnesses." There was an unmistakable hint of hostility in his voice.

Dev nodded. "Yes," he said. "That's the idea. Your consciousnesses have already been digitized, so it's the quickest way to get it done."

"And what makes you think any of us would agree to that? Presumptuous of you, isn't it?"

"Actually," Dev said with a hint of defensiveness, "one of you has already agreed to it."

A look of genuine shock flashed across Brian's face. "Who?"

Dev's eyes flashed back to his father, and Rajeev nodded, consenting to the disclosure Dev was about to give. It's not like he had much of a choice, anyway; Dev's glance his way was enough to give it away.

"My dad," he said.

All eyes turned to Rajeev, including Natalie's, who seemed particularly caught off guard by the announcement; if anyone should have known before everyone else, it was her.

"Is that true, Rajeev?" Brian asked.

Rajeev nodded. "It's not an idea that I relish," he said. "The thought of my consciousness, my essence, mingling with some soulless artificial intelligence in some hastily conceived science experiment … it's a notion that fills me to the brim with existential dread. But I honestly believe it's a necessary evil if we want to stop Daniel."

Brian furrowed his brow and looked like he was about to argue, but he shook his head and his face softened. He offered a shrug. "It's your mind," he said. "I suppose you can do what you want with it."

Rajeev flashed him a wry smile. "Thanks for your permission."

"Anyway," Dev said, "the point is that we have a real, potentially viable plan to stop Daniel. We'd like to explore other options that aren't so, uh … ethically ambiguous … but we'll work to have this option queued up and ready to go at a moment's notice." He scanned his head, making eye contact with everyone in the group. "Does that alleviate the concern I'm hearing?"

The room filled with soft chattering, and eventually everyone's eyes gravitated to Brian who had become the impromptu voice of the original concern. He pondered a moment, then nodded.

"At least it's something," he said.

"It's more than something," Maltek said a bit combatively. "I, for one, think we should ditch the alternatives and go right to the AI-human hybrid. If we're going to take this monster out, we need to take risks."

Dev shook his head. "While I appreciate your enthusiasm, Gregory, I think the cautious approach is the right one for now—and I suspect the majority of the others would agree with that, given the ethical considerations at play. Is that right?" He waited a moment to gauge the reaction, which mostly came in the form of affirmative nods. "If we're in agreement then, you can all try to relax a bit. Gregory and I, on the other hand, don't have that luxury. We have a lot of work to do." He

NINETEEN

turned to face Maltek. "Let's get to it."

Twenty

After Dev adjourned the meeting, Natalie sidled up next to Rajeev and placed her hand in his. He couldn't help the grin that grew across his face.

"I was wondering if you'd like to go on a walk with me," she said.

"A walk? We're in the middle of nowhere."

She smiled. "Perfect. I could use a little time out in unperverted nature, away from all … *this.*"

" 'This'?"

"This … overload of technology. Android bodies, exoskeletons, computer programs, and renegade virtual assistants out for blood. I could use a break from it all. Well, except for the android body. I can't really help that."

Rajeev smiled. He had never been much of a nature lover—he'd lived in large cities his entire life—but he had to admit that Natalie made a compelling point about the outsize influence of technology in their lives … particularly as it pertained to their present problems. Getting away from it all, even if just for an hour or two, sounded heavenly … especially with such enchanting company.

"Sure," he said. "Let's do it."

They marched up the steep steps leading out of the underground bunker that had been their home for so long and emerged into the lush, green woods. It almost felt like awakening from a dream or coming out of a coma—a sensation with which Rajeev was all too familiar.

"A girl could get used to this," Natalie said. "I have half a mind to leave everything behind and run off to live in the woods."

"Well, that's not an option," Rajeev said. "So let's make the most of the opportunity while we can, before we have to head back."

They walked hand in hand through the forest, taking in the vibrant green foliage and basking in the calls of birds and other wildlife. A light breeze whipped against their skin as they walked, rustling the leaves of the surrounding trees. The perilous threat that Daniel represented seemed to fade into the background as they strode farther and farther away from the bunker, until the thought escaped their memory altogether and they walked around truly in blind bliss, enraptured by the nature that surrounded them and by each other's company.

A deer pranced out in front of them and they stopped in their tracks; a gasp escaped Natalie's artificial lips. The deer turned and looked at them, offering the same blank stare it would have exhibited if it had been staring down a pair of headlights, then bounced back into the woods as if nothing had happened.

"Did you see how close it got?" Natalie exclaimed.

Rajeev laughed. "Yes, I did. Too bad I don't have a gun with me. We could have had fresh venison for dinner."

Natalie slugged his shoulder playfully. "That's horrible, Rajeev!"

"Hey, relax! It was a joke. It's not like we can even eat anyway!"

Eventually they came to a small pond. They found a fallen log and took a seat on it, watching out over the peaceful pond scene and enjoying the tranquil landscape before them. Natalie leaned her head on Rajeev's shoulder, and he placed an arm around her waist, pulling her close to him.

"I'm so glad I got the opportunity to know you," she said.

He smiled. "Oh yeah?"

She smiled back. "Yeah. I mean, I was not looking for any kind of romance at the Next Level Technologies headquarters. But isn't it always the way it goes that romance finds you when you're least expecting it?"

Rajeev nodded. "I can commiserate. I definitely wasn't looking to get involved with anyone so soon after discovering Sarah was with someone else. I was heartbroken, and yet, it felt inevitable that I move on. I just didn't think it would happen so quickly."

Their eyes met, and for a moment, they were lost in each other. The nature surrounding them faded into the background and as far as they were concerned, they may as well have been in Rajeev's dorm. He leaned forward and pressed his lips to hers. She kissed him back, and they wrapped their arms around each other, pulling their bodies close.

He lifted her up, never breaking their embrace, and lowered her to the ground. The hardness of the ground didn't matter; they had transcended the material plane of existence. As they hastily removed each other's clothes and burned their passion brighter, they left this world behind completely and embraced oblivion.

Twenty-One

Reality seeped back into their brains, and as they lay curled up in each other's arms, they realized the day was growing short and that they should head back to the bunker. Rajeev planted one last kiss on Natalie's cheek. "Come on," he said. "Let's get dressed."

She let out an exaggerated groan. "Do we *have* to?"

Rajeev chuckled. "Well, we have to eventually. How about five more minutes?"

She snuggled into him. "It'll have to do."

Neither of them wanted to break their reverie. Five minutes turned to ten, and ten to fifteen, but before it could hit twenty, Rajeev nudged his paramour away.

"Come on," he said. "Let's go. If we wait any longer we'll be walking back in the dark."

Natalie resisted for a moment, but her hesitation was brief. With a dissatisfied groan, she acquiesced to Rajeev's request. She stood and began to dress. When each of them was once again fully clothed, they started the journey back to the bunker. They walked slowly, even as the sun began to set, eager to prolong their respite from their troubles for as long as possible.

"I wish we could stay out here, together, forever," Natalie said.

"Don't say that," Rajeev said.

"Why not?"

He'd said the words reflexively, and it took him a moment to sort through the flurry of emotions that had led him to speak them. In truth, he wished they could stay out here forever as well, and that's why he didn't want the desire spoken aloud: He might be tempted to give in.

"Because it's not possible," he told her.

She didn't say anything to that, but it was clear from the way she pursed her lips that she wasn't happy with his response, even if, deep down, she agreed with it. He wished he hadn't said anything at all.

They approached the towering monolith that marked the entrance to the bunker. As they descended, they felt a little bit of peace fade away with each step. Their short trip away had refreshed them to a degree, but as they made their way closer to the heart of their current home, they couldn't help but be reminded of all the chaos they'd come from, and all of the chaos that still awaited them.

* * *

Natalie and Rajeev parted ways and retreated to their respective dormitories. Rajeev had barely begun making himself comfortable when Dev popped in.

"I need to talk to you," he said. He hadn't knocked; there was none of the usual politeness that typically accompanied his presence.

"Okay," Rajeev said with a nod. "Just let me get settled and I'll—"

"I need to talk to you now. It's urgent."

Rajeev felt a pit form in his stomach. What now? He'd barely returned from his all-to-brief break from all of this, and here he was already being thrust right back into thick of all the craziness that had come to so thoroughly dominate their lives. Somehow, the short reprieve had actually managed to make things worse; he felt like he was on the verge of experiencing a panic attack at the slightest provocation.

"Okay," he said. "Let's talk."

"Follow me," Dev said, and he turned and walked away without even waiting to see if his father would follow. Rajeev stood and followed Dev out of the dorm. His son led him to his office, where Maltek was already seated and waiting inside. Rajeev couldn't help but feel like a little kid who was about to get a stern talking to from his parents.

"Take a seat, dad."

Rajeev did so, then looked up at his son pensively. "What's going on?"

Dev turned to Maltek. They stared at each other for a moment that felt longer than it was. Finally, Maltek nodded, and he took the reins of the conversation. "We've had some time to go over the data that was corrupted due to Daniel's data breach," he said. Rajeev expected him to keep speaking, but he'd paused.

"Yeah?" Rajeev asked. "Was it that bad?"

There was a moment of silence, as both Dev and Maltek avoided answering the question. Just as Dev's lips parted and it seemed he was about to say something, Rajeev was blasted by an emergency alert; he could tell by the startled look on his companions' faces that they had received the same alert on their AR glasses.

Before he could even finish reading the alert, Rajeev could tell it was bad. And he had a good guess who was responsible: Daniel.

Twenty-Two

Thus far, Daniel's mayhem had been confined to limited geographic regions. He'd been testing the waters, seeing what he was capable of. Dev, Maltek and Rajeev all knew he was capable of much more than what he'd done so far. And now it seemed he was finally taking advantage of his full strength.

Reports were flooding in of "glitches" and "malfunctions" all over the country. Cars were driving off roads, thermostats were cranking themselves up as far as they could go, lawnmowers were mowing down people instead of grass; machines were turning against their owners like some 1950s-era pulp sci-fi novel's vision of the apocalypse.

But there was one incident in particular that had summed up the extent of what was happening, that illustrated that the country was facing a threat like nothing it had ever faced before, and which, if left unchecked, would undoubtedly spread and menace the entire world: The White House had been destroyed. Every news organization's video streams were focused on the image of bright orange flames arising from the ashes of what had once been one of the country's foremost symbols of democracy. It was unclear whether the president had escaped before the building had been attacked, but it didn't much matter. Daniel had sent a message, and everyone in the country had received it: Things would never be the same.

Dev, Maltek and Rajeev stood silently for a moment, stunned by the broadcast they were seeing. When Rajeev finally spoke, his voice sounded small.

"What do we do? What *can* we do?"

Dev and Maltek shared a look. It was a brief look, but apparently conveyed a wealth of information, and in that moment Rajeev realized that despite all odds, Maltek and his son had become friends ... or at least, something resembling friendship had blossomed between them. Perhaps he shouldn't have been so surprised. They had been forced to work together to save humanity, working long, grueling hours side by side. They had been bonded together by fate in much the same way soldiers are bonded together by war. Despite the terrible things Maltek—the original incarnation of Maltek, anyway—had done in the past, it appeared some good had come out of it, perhaps. Rajeev wondered if Maltek was deserving of forgiveness. Then again, did he even require forgiveness? Technically, the man standing before them was just a copy of Maltek's mind, in the same way Rajeev was a copy of a man who had lived and lost a separate life. Likewise, could the version of Maltek standing before them really be held responsible for the actions of a man who shared a mind with him, but not a past? So far, the only actions they had to judge him on were good—he had offered indispensable help in their fight against Daniel. But Rajeev feared that something sinister might be lingering in the clone's psyche, and he worried that the friendship blossoming between him and his son may be a pretense for some sinister agenda.

Rajeev's flurry of thoughts was interrupted by Dev answering his question.

"I don't know," he said softly. "Where can we even start? The entire country is in chaos."

"What do you think his goal is?" Rajeev asked. "Is he trying to control us? Destroy us? Does he think he's trying to protect us in some twisted way, like something out of an Asimov novel?"

"Does it matter?" Maltek asked. "Whether it's A, B, C, or all of the above, it's bad news for the human species."

"Maybe it's time for the killswitch," Rajeev said.

"Killswitch?" Dev asked, his eyes growing wide. "You mean—

Rajeev nodded. "Pulling the plug on the internet all together."

"That's risky," Maltek said. "It may already be too late. For all we know, Daniel's already set up his own servers and equipment and shielded them in EMP-proof Faraday cages. We might blow up the internet for nothing."

"It could at least slow him down," Rajeev offered. "Better he be contained to a few servers he's managed to cobble together than to … everything."

"Okay," Maltek said. "As a last resort, maybe it's better than nothing. But there's still another option."

"Merging a copy of my consciousness with your AI," Rajeev said.

Maltek nodded. "Yes."

There was an awkward silence, and Maltek turned and stared at Dev, whose eyes drifted down to look at his feet.

"That's actually what we had come to talk to you about," he said.

"Oh? I thought you were going to talk to me about the data breach?"

Dev let out a long sigh. "The data breach did a lot more damage than we initially thought, and much of it is unrecoverable … including the copies of everyone's consciousnesses that we had stored."

"We were going to ask you to let us copy your mind again," Maltek said. "But with this latest attack by Daniel, I don't think we have time for that anymore."

"Then we have to shut it down," Rajeev said. "We have to take down the internet. If that's the only option, then so be it. The alternative is that Daniel takes over everything."

"Stop and think about what that would really mean," Maltek said. "The internet governs nearly every facet of our society. Destroying the internet would mean the collapse of the entire electrical grid. It would mean taking millions of people in hospitals off life support in seconds. It would mean kneecapping our ability to produce and transport food."

"I know all that," Rajeev said. "But it's still better than the alternative."

"I'm not saying it shouldn't still be on the table as a last resort. But merging your consciousness with the AI still might work, with the added benefit of not destroying modern civilization as we know it."

"But you two just told me that wasn't possible."

"No," Maltek said. "We told you it wasn't possible to merge a *copy* of your consciousness."

"Yeah, that's—"

Maltek's words settled in Rajeev's brain, and as the meaning of those words sunk in, Rajeev's face fell. If he'd had blood, it would have run cold. He looked Maltek directly in the eyes, then turned to his son. He couldn't hide the shock or the pain that was surely displayed on his face.

"You're saying you want *me* to merge with the AI. Not a copy of myself, but the version standing before you right now, with no backup, no duplicate on hand to restore me to my present state. You're asking me, in effect, to sacrifice myself."

Dev turned away; Maltek nodded gravely.

"I wish it wasn't so," he said, "but that's exactly what I'm saying."

Twenty-Three

You don't have to do this, dad. In fact, I'm telling you not to. We'll find another way to stop Daniel."

"There isn't another way!" Maltek shouted. His eyes met Dev's and, seeing the pain in his eyes, Maltek's voice softened when he spoke again. "I'm sorry. I wish there was, too. Maybe there could be, if we had more time. But we don't. Daniel is making his move *now*. We don't have time to figure something else out, and we can't risk pulling the plug on the entire 'net. This is our best hope. This is our *only* hope."

Rajeev didn't respond. He couldn't respond; he could barely comprehend what was being asked of him.

"He's my *dad*," Dev spat.

"Fine," Maltek said. "It doesn't have to be him, specifically." He gestured toward the rest of the bunker, toward the dormitories. "Any of them will do just fine. But we can't sit here and debate it all day. We have to act, and we have to act now."

At this, Rajeev bristled. The thought that one of the other androids might be put in harm's way because he refused to step up was intolerable to him. The very suggestion of it crystallized his resolve. The idea of sacrificing himself no longer seemed quite so crazy.

"Okay," he said, his voice now firm, confident. He nodded. "I'll do it."

"Dad—no," Dev said. "You don't have to—"

"I'm sure as hell not going to let anyone else do it in my place," Rajeev interjected. "And it seems, as Maltek has made abundantly clear, that we're all out of other options. So unfortunately, Dev, you're wrong. I do have to do this."

Dev's face contorted in pain. Rajeev could only imagine what he was going through. He'd lost his father at a young age, and spent his entire life working to bring him back. And he'd done it. He'd defied the odds and found a way to bring his father out of a coma and give him a second chance at life. But he hadn't really even gotten to enjoy the fruit of his labor. After escaping imprisonment, Dev and Rajeev had been embroiled in one battle after another. They hadn't had time to renew their relationship as father and son; instead, they'd acted more as fellow soldiers. They'd believed the sacrifice was worth it, that they were working toward a future where the existential threats they faced would be defeated and they could live their lives as father and son once more. But now, finally and irrevocably, that dream was being wrested from their hands. No, Rajeev would not be going away completely, but there was no telling what would happen when his consciousness merged with the AI. Maybe he'd still be there in some halfway recognizable form, but there was an equally likely chance he'd be so thoroughly assimilated that any trace of an entity known as Rajeev Sundaram would cease to exist.

Tears ran down Dev's face. Rajeev's lip trembled. He was transported back to a time before he'd woken up in this alien future, to a time when Dev had been just a boy and fallen off his bicycle, skinning his knees. He'd come rushing into the house, tears flowing, in so much distress he couldn't even find words between the sobs to express what was wrong. But Rajeev knew. In that moment, his parental instincts had kicked in and his sole mission in life was to comfort and care for his son. Now, all these years later, whether he was truly Rajeev or just a faint shadow, his mission was the same.

He rushed forward and wrapped his arms around his son, and even though his body was made of silicon and silicone, in that moment, they felt each other's heartbeats.

"Dev," he said, half-whispering into his son's ear as they embraced, "I know it's not just me making this sacrifice." He hugged him tighter, then released the embrace so he could look his son in the eyes. "But a father doesn't have a choice. I can't allow my son and daughter to live in a world where they're dead or enslaved, even if it means sacrificing myself. If you have a child someday, you'll recognize and realize that you would make the same choice if you were in my shoes today."

"I don't mean to break up the moment," Maltek said, "but if you've made a final decision—and I wholeheartedly believe it's the right decision—then we need to get on with it. We're running out of time."

Rajeev turned to Dev, who was drying his tears with the sleeve of his shirt. When he'd gotten most of them, he looked up at his father and offered a reluctant nod.

"Okay," Rajeev said. "You two get things ready on your end. I'll be back in ten minutes. I have to go say some goodbyes."

Twenty-Four

Every step Rajeev took as he exited Dev's office and made his way toward Natalie's dormitory felt like it took an eternity. His mind was abuzz with more thoughts than he could process. The last few moments had been surreal. It felt like the conversation with Dev and Maltek had taken place in a faraway dream, not an immediate reality.

By the time he reached Natalie's room, he was filled with dread; not from his impending fate, which he was beginning to resign himself to, but rather over the fact that he would have to deliver the devastating news to her—news he was certain would crush, if not destroy, her. He delivered three slow, hard knocks, and waited for her to answer.

When the door opened, Natalie looked tired, but happy. But as her eyes fell upon Rajeev's distressed face, her expression mirrored his.

"What's wrong?" He pushed past her and took a seat on her bed. She followed him, taking a seat beside him and grasping his hands, pulling them to her chest. "Rajeev, what is it? Is this about the news reports that came in about Daniel?"

Rajeev shook his head as he worked up the courage to speak the words he needed to say to her. Finally, he did so.

"During the data breach, Daniel apparently destroyed a lot more data than Dev and Maltek had initially thought," he began. "Among the data that was lost were all the copies Dev had stored of our consciousnesses."

Natalie shrugged. "So we'll make new copies," she said.

"Yes. You and the other androids can and should get new copies made as backups. But we're facing a dire, immediate threat from Daniel now, and to fight him, Dev and Maltek need a digitized consciousness to merge with their AI."

"Okay … so they can copy your—"

"There's no time to do any copying. It's a complicated process. It takes hours. We can't wait that long."

"Then … then what are we supposed to …" as she spoke, a look of realization spread across her face.

"They're going to merge my consciousness with the AI," he said. "Not a copy. Me. The me that is here now and talking to you."

"You can't," she exclaimed. "No. You can't do this."

"It's not something I'm looking forward to. But it can't be helped. There's no other way to stop Daniel … at least, not without a massive amount of collateral damage."

"But Rajeev, I—"

"I'm sorry," Rajeev interrupted. "But this is the only way. The fate of humanity is at stake. How can I put my one life in the way of saving the lives of billions of others?"

"But I … I *need* you," she gasped.

The desperation in her voice melted Rajeev's heart. He hugged her, and as he held her tightly to his body, he leaned his head down to plant a kiss atop her head. "I need you too," he said. "And if I don't do this, I won't have you. You'll be subjected to a robotic tyranny that will either rule over or exterminate you. We all will. But if I do this, if I can stop him, then you'll go on living. True, it will be with a broken heart, at least for a while. But time will heal you, and you will go on living. You will meet someone new. You will love again. And every once in a while the memory of me will pop into your head, and you'll smile and be grateful that I made this sacrifice so you could live that life."

She pulled away from him and shook her head violently. "I don't want that life! I want *you*, here, now!"

"I want that too. But it's out of our hands. There's nothing we can do at this point. But at least I can do something to stop this kind of heartache from sweeping through all of humanity—because that's what will happen if someone doesn't step up to stop Daniel."

He stood, and beckoned for her to stand as well and approach him. She did so, and he bent down and pressed his lips to hers forcefully, as if he were trying to stamp a lasting imprint on them, a reminder of him she could carry with her long after he was gone.

Their lips parted, and he stared into her eyes. "I love you," he said. He placed the back of his hand against her cheek. "I was so lost when I awoke from that coma and found myself in that crude android body. And you're one of the things that helped me find myself again. I'll always be grateful to you for that."

She looked up at him, her face contorted in absolute pain, but also the beginning of resignation. "I love you too, Rajeev. I will never, ever forget you. I need you to know that."

He kissed her again. "I know," he said. "And I need you to know that no matter what becomes of me when the merge is complete, I will never forget you, either. No matter how deeply it may be buried, some part of that new entity will still be me, and I will never stop thinking of you. I will never stop loving you. I promise you that."

Twenty-Five

When Rajeev knocked on Mira's door, he felt calmer than he had before approaching Natalie. Breaking the news to her, embracing her and grieving with her, had been cathartic. He was grateful for that, because he knew this news was going to be hard on his daughter and he needed to be strong for her.

The door swung open. Mira's eyes were wide.

"Dad! Did you see the news?"

"About Daniel, you mean? Yes, I saw it."

"What are we going to do?"

"We have a plan to address it. That's kind of what I wanted to talk to you about. May I come in?"

She stepped aside to allow him to enter. He didn't bother sitting down; time was running out and he'd be leaving again in just a few short moments.

"It appears we've run out of options," he said. "Daniel is making his final attack, and the only option left on the table that might actually be capable of stopping him is to merge my consciousness with the AI."

"Okay," Mira said. "Well, we were all prepared for that possibility anyway. How soon do you think Dev and Maltek can have the new version of the AI up and running?"

Here we go, Rajeev thought. He took a deep breath. "It's not that simple. When Daniel attacked our servers and corrupted much of the data Dev had stored, he—"

Rajeev was interrupted by a shrill, piercing siren that suddenly shot through the compound. He and Mira glanced at each other and without hesitation, they rushed out of the room to see what was going on. Red lights that Rajeev had never even realized were there flashed from the ceiling, casting an eerie, hellish glow over the compound.

The other dorms emptied out, and soon everyone was standing around, panicked, awaiting news from anyone who could tell them what was going on. After a moment, Dev and Maltek came running out of the office.

"Daniel is attacking," Dev shouted.

"We know that already!" Brian shouted back. "We all saw the same broadcasts."

"That's not what I mean." Dev's voice had taken on a bit of testiness at being challenged. "Daniel is *here*, right now. He's attacking the bunker. One of the security drones we have looking out for threats spotted a large group of androids heading this way. They'll be here in minutes." Gasps broke out throughout the group; Dev raised his hands to silence them. "We're moving straight to merging my dad's consciousness with the AI. But while Maltek and I get that set up, we're going to need all of your help to keep Daniel and his army at bay until we can take the fight to cyberspace."

Instantly, the faces of everyone in the group, human and android alike, hardened. Panic gave way to resolve. Their lives, and in fact, the very existence of the human race, may be imperiled, but if this was to be their last stand, they would give it everything they had. They would not meet their end today.

"Everyone find an exoskeleton to use," Dev commanded the humans; the androids, of course, were already equipped with bodies made for combat. "The more firepower the better. Then surround the entrance to the bunker and fight off the intruders for as long as you can. We'll try to work as quickly as we can down here. We can do this. We'll win this war."

With that, the group dispersed to spend the precious little time they had left to prepare for battle. When Mira caught sight of her father walking back to the office with Dev and Maltek, however, she realized something was wrong.

"Dad, what are you doing?"

He turned around to face her. Dev stopped as well, but Maltek kept walking without so much as looking over his shoulder.

Rajeev and Dev shared a look. "Can you give us a minute?" Rajeev asked.

Dev nodded solemnly. "Of course. Maltek and I will go get ready. Come when you're ready … but don't take too long." He walked off, leaving Rajeev alone with his daughter.

Mira looked up at him with a look of concern. "What's going on?"

"Mira … the data breach destroyed all the copies Dev had stored of people's consciousnesses."

"I don't see what that has to do with—"

"Mira, *I* am the consciousness they're going to merge with the AI."

"What? You mean—" She stopped short of finishing the sentence; the look on Rajeev's face had already answered her question in the affirmative.

"Dad," she said, her eyes filling with tears, "we just got you back. Now we're going to lose you again?"

He stepped forward and embraced her, holding her tight, and even though she was a fully grown woman, he felt like he was holding his baby girl in his arms.

"I know it's hard," he said. "But the alternative is doing nothing and creating a world where my children are dead, or at the very least, not free. And I couldn't live with myself if I did nothing when I could have provided a better world for you."

Her tears flowed heavily now. "Isn't there another way?" she croaked out between sobs.

"I wish there was," he said. "But Dev went over every other possibility and this is our best shot. If there'd been more time, perhaps he could have made another copy of my mind. But there isn't time. Destruction is literally at our door, and we have to act fast." He kissed her cheek. "I love you so much, Mira. Now you go out there and you fight with all your might. Be the strong woman I know you are. Fight, and win."

Mira pulled back and wiped away her tears. She looked up at her father and her face grew firm, determined. "I will."

Twenty-Six

When Rajeev returned to Dev's office, Maltek was working at the computer as Dev was setting up the interface that would connect his father to the computer and the AI.

"I'm just about done," Dev said, sparing only a slight glance his father's way before turning back to his work. "Take a seat and I'll get you hooked up in just a moment."

Rajeev took a seat and waited for Dev to finish up. He was slightly taken aback by how detached Dev was acting—he was all business—but then, he imagined he was suppressing any strong emotions he may be feeling to focus on the task at hand. Maybe, Rajeev thought, Dev was afraid that if he focused too much on what was about to happen, he wouldn't have the strength to go through with it. For his part, Rajeev wasn't sure he could go through with it if he thought too hard about it, either. Dev approached him and lowered a bowl-like device with coils of wires protruding from it onto Rajeev's head. It looked like it had been hobbled together, but Rajeev had trust in his son's technical prowess.

"This is similar to the devices we use to duplicate consciousnesses for our android bodies," Dev said. "But I've modified this one so instead of scanning and copying your consciousness, it will create a live interface between your mind and the computer. The program Maltek and I have been working on will merge your consciousness with our AI."

"Will it be instant? Or will the process be drawn out?"

"It will take some time," Dev answered. "Maltek and I will need to initiate the program, and it's more complicated than merely flipping a switch. Once the merge is initiated, we expect there to be an acclimation period in which each consciousness integrates the other into itself. This has never been done before, so we don't know exactly how long that process will take. Further, we don't even know for sure what the end result is going to be. Like we've said, the hope is that we can remove the manual constraints we've put on the AI, and that your human consciousness will restrain it instead."

"Okay." Rajeev wanted to pinch himself. It didn't feel like what was happening was real. He was awaiting some grand new frontier he could barely fathom. Like death, he had no idea what awaited him on the other side of the procedure. He turned to his son as he finished up fastening the device to his head via a chin strap. "Dev?"

"Yeah, dad?"

"I want you to know that I love you."

Dev stopped and looked in his father's eyes. "I know you do, dad."

"And tell your mom … tell her I love her, also. I didn't get a chance to say goodbye to her. But I want her to know that I harbor absolutely zero ill will against her for moving on. I'm happy that she's happy. She should know that."

Dev stifled a tear. "I'll tell her, dad."

"Okay. Let's do this then. I just hope our guys can hold off Daniel long enough for you and Maltek to do your thing."

* * *

As the androids and the exoskeleton-wielding humans emerged from the bunker and trudged up the steps to the forest, they were met with inky blackness. It was nearly eleven at night, and the opaqueness of the dark lent a sinister atmosphere to the fight they knew was coming.

Thankfully, the android bodies were equipped with low-light vision, and it didn't even need to be activated. Natalie found that her vision adjusted automatically, and although it was a gradual process, she could see just fine within a few short minutes.

The humans in the exoskeletons didn't have the benefit of such built-in features, but they'd had the foresight to don full-head helmets that had been among the bunker's inventory. The helmets' visors included night-vision capability, which put the humans on mostly even footing with their android counterparts.

As they came to the top of the stairs, they spread out and formed a perimeter around the bunker's entrance and waited. So far there was no sign of Daniel's army, but they knew they were near. They'd be at their doorstep soon enough. Natalie felt a rush reminiscent of an adrenaline boost course through her body; it must have been some part of the algorithms governing her mind's relationship with her body in a manner that simulated the processes of an organic body. She welcomed it. It made her alert, responsive; she knew she could spring into action at the drop of a pin if the situation required it.

They stood vigilant in the darkness, erect and unmoving like ancient sentinels, as they waited for their enemies to appear. Every now and then, a cool breeze swirled through; if they'd had human bodies, or lacked the protection of the exoskeletons, it would have chilled them. But as it was, the breeze was merely a slight annoyance. They remained upright, still as statues, diligent and patient.

And then they saw them. It was just a handful of them at first—bodies emerging from behind trees and making their way toward the bunker. But the small smattering soon gave way to dozens, and then hundreds, their faces blank, their bodies moving with an eerie, mechanical precision that was completely inhuman. As Natalie looked on, it occurred to her that she was looking at Daniel. He occupied each and every one of the bodies before them. They were not so much individuals as appendages controlled by the mind that was Daniel. He was their Queen, and they were his drones.

The androids at the front line stopped twenty feet or so from the bunker's entrance and waited, staring straight ahead with blank, emotionless stares. Natalie and the rest of her comrades stared back, but not lifelessly; the expressions on their faces ranged from scared, to concerned, to excited.

Natalie had expected one of the androids to step forward and address them, but none did. Instead, to her surprise, the androids all opened their mouths simultaneously and spoke as one:

"Let us pass."

Hearing hundreds of androids speak in perfect unison was one of the strangest things Natalie had ever experienced. She looked around the group, and everyone else was registering the same shock on their faces. No one knew quite how to respond, so no one did.

The androids spoke again: "Let us pass." There was no hint of impatience in their inflection, nor upon their faces. It was just a dispassionate order that had been released into the air.

Natalie waited a moment for someone to respond. When no one did, she took a step forward and spoke for the group.

"No!" she shouted. "Daniel! We are not against you, but we cannot let you pass. Please, just turn around and go."

There was no reaction at first. The seconds rolled by and it appeared Daniel was contemplating the words Natalie had spoken. As they waited almost a full minute for Daniel to react, Natalie began to think that perhaps the virtual assistant was stuck in some kind of feedback loop, unable to retreat *or* advance.

But she was mistaken. At that moment, the lead android lurched toward them and continued its march forward. Half a second later, the rest of the android army followed suit, following their leader as they marched toward the enemy.

Whatever Natalie's robotic equivalent to blood was, it had run cold. She glanced left and right to her compatriots and nodded. They nodded back. Collectively, they dug in their heels and raised their fists, bracing themselves.

The war with Daniel had come to their doorstep, and they were ready for the fight.

Twenty-Seven

O kay," Maltek said. "I just initiated the program. It's going to take about ten minutes for it to map out both your brain and the AI and figure out how to combine them. Then it will start the process of merging the two of you together."

"How long will that take?" Rajeev asked.

Maltek shrugged. "Your guess is as good as mine."

Rajeev lowered his head and looked at his feet. He closed his eyes and took in a deep breath. "I'm anxious," he said.

"I don't blame you," Dev said. "I'm really sorry, dad. I never intended for you to be made into a Guinea pig."

Rajeev offered a sad smile. "It's not your fault, Dev."

"That's not entirely true. I created Daniel in the first place. It's my fault he's wreaking all this havoc."

"It's a good thing you created Daniel. If you hadn't, then Maltek would have taken over." He glanced over Dev's shoulder at Maltek. "No offense."

Maltek smirked. "None taken."

Rajeev continued. "Unleashing Daniel was a necessary evil, but we're going to undo the damage. None of us is happy with this sacrifice, me least of all, but I take solace in the fact that I'll be helping countless others. I hope you'll take solace in that too."

Tears formed in Dev's eyes. "I'll try," he choked out.

The three of them fell into silence, lost in their respective thoughts and emotions. Rajeev had almost forgotten what they were doing when he was suddenly reminded by what he could only describe as an acute pressure in his mind.

"Something's happening," he said, a slight edge of panic in his voice.

Dev and Maltek perked up. "What is it?" Dev asked.

"I … I don't know. My mind feels … different. I guess the program must be working."

"Don't try to fight it," Maltek said.

Dev nodded. "I know it probably goes against your instincts, but Maltek is right; the more you're able to relax, the easier the union will be."

"Union," Rajeev repeated. "Makes it sound like a marriage."

"I guess it kind of is, in a sense," Dev said. "Two becoming one."

"Except usually the groom is excited about it."

"I'm not sure that's true, actually," Dev said with a laugh.

Rajeev laughed as well. "Fair enough," he said. "Maybe it's an apt comparison after all."

His mind was jolted by another bout of pressure, and he winced; the sensation wasn't painful, per se, but it was immensely uncomfortable.

"Are you okay, dad?"

"I'm fine," he said. "It's just … it feels like my mind is a fortress, and some enemy force is at the gates trying to barge its way in."

"Try to let it in as much as possible," Dev said. "Embrace it, even."

Rajeev gritted his teeth. "I don't know if I can."

"It's okay," Dev said. "Try your best."

Rajeev's hands found their way to his temples; the gesture didn't do much to alleviate his discomfort, but it provided at least a modicum of psychological support for what he was going through. He felt an alien presence chipping away at his mind, and he was afraid of losing himself to it. But then, that was the whole point of this exercise, wasn't it? If he'd been stronger, he would have given up without a fight and let the program do whatever it wanted. But he couldn't help but fight. Some ancient instinct embedded deep in his mind was at work enacting a solitary objective: Survive at any cost.

Dev tried to put on a brave face, but he couldn't completely hide the sadness that had crept into his eyes. It pained him to see what his father was going through. He wondered if this was what it was like to watch a loved one go through chemotherapy, only in a way, this was even worse—chemo tended to help cancer patients get better, whereas the process Rajeev was going through would almost certainly mean Dev would lose him forever.

He placed a comforting hand on his dad's shoulder, but Rajeev barely seemed to notice. His eyes were clasped shut in apparent pain, and although his android body didn't sweat, Dev got the sense that if he'd had pores, his forehead would have been covered in a thick sheen of perspiration.

"Hang in there," Dev said in what he hoped was an encouraging voice. "You're doing great."

Upon hearing his son's words, Rajeev looked up and opened his eyes. What Dev saw in them sent a chill through his spine. The pain, thankfully, appeared to have disappeared completely; Rajeev's body had relaxed and he no longer clenched his jaw or balled his hands into fists. But his eyes looked somehow both empty and faraway. Dev could tell immediately that the presence staring at him through those dead eyes was not his father—not completely, anyway.

Then, like an animatronic toy that had been switched off, Rajeev's body slumped in the chair, suddenly devoid of all life.

"What happened?" Maltek asked in an awed whisper.

Dev shook his head. "I'm not sure."

Twenty-Eight

Natalie was able to easily dispatch the first of Daniel's androids that came her way. Although Daniel's mind was vast, it appeared that spreading his consciousness over hundreds or thousands of bodies had diluted their individual capacity for cognition. The androids were incapable of any kind of complex combat maneuvers; the best they could do was rush forward and attempt to tackle anyone—or anything—that stood in their way. So when the first combatant made its way to Natalie, all she had to do was stick out her arm and propel it into the android's head to send it crumpled onto the ground.

It soon became apparent that this strategy wouldn't hold up over time; what Daniel's androids lacked in skill they more than made up for in sheer numbers, and there was no way their small group would be able to take them on hand-to-hand.

Apparently one of her compatriots was thinking the same thing. One of the humans had discovered that the exoskeleton they were wearing was equipped with built-in rockets. They pointed their arm into the crowd of oncoming androids and shot the projectile into the heart of it. There was a brilliant burst of flame, and as it cleared the crowd appeared to have been thinned considerably. But Natalie could already tell that the respite from the onslaught would be short-lived. They needed to repeat the rocket action again if they were going to continue to hold their own.

"Everyone capable of firing rockets, take aim at the crowd," she shouted. "Don't fire right away. Wait for them to come closer, then take turns firing one at a time. Let's hold them off that way as long as we can and take out as many as possible!"

It took the enemy androids about a minute to regroup and continue their advance. When they were just a matter of feet from the entrance to the bunker, another explosion rocked them, blowing those at the front of the line apart.

"Good job!" Natalie shouted. "Now get ready for the next one!"

They repeated the process three more times. As the smoke on the third strike dissipated, Natalie grew disheartened. Each attack had the desired effect of clearing out the mass of attacking androids, but each time the throng on the outskirts quickly moved up to fill the space once occupied by their fallen comrades. They couldn't keep this up forever; the rockets were a finite resource; the androids, she feared, were less so.

She glanced over at Brian, and when she caught his attention she expressed her concern. "Are these things ever going to let up?"

"They have to eventually," he shouted back.

"I know that. But are we going to run out of rockets before Daniel runs out of bodies? What then?"

A rocket went off; after bracing for the explosion, he turned back to Natalie. "We won't take them all out, obviously. But we'll take a good lot of 'em out, and we should be able to take on the remnants hand-to-hand."

"Are you sure about that?"

Brian's brow furrowed. "No." He shrugged and turned back to the army of androids reassembling before him.

Natalie hoped Brian was right, that when all the smoke had cleared and all the dust had settled, they'd be on equal footing with the androids that remained. But, just like Brian, she couldn't be sure that was the case. An image popped into her mind of dozens of Daniel's androids swarming over her, forcing her onto the ground; in the vision, she was able to throw them off of her, but others lurched forward to replace them, until they'd piled up so high on top of her that she was crushed underneath their weight and they tore her apart.

She shook her head, dispelling the dark thought from her mind. It was useless to dwell on the worst-case scenario. She should be prepared for the worst, but be hoping—and focusing on—the best.

"How many rockets are left?"

"I've got two left," Mira shouted.

The rest of the group shouted out their answers, and Natalie kept track of the math in her head. When they'd all answered, she added the numbers up to reach the total: There were five rockets left.

Five rockets. That's all that stood between them and a throng of robotic supersoldiers.

She took in the sight of the androids and tried to determine how many were left. It was difficult to tell. The trees obscured their view of the androids that were farthest away. It was clear that there were currently too many for them to fight; but would that still be true after five more rocket blasts?

It was anyone's guess.

One. The conflagration lit up the darkness. New androids quickly rushed forward to fill in the gaps left by their exploded brethren.

Two. Another explosion; another cascade of shredded android body parts flying through the air. And no end in sight to the onslaught.

Three. A sense of dread crept into Natalie's countenance. She had never been a particularly religious woman, but as she watched the crowd of androids fill back in, she found herself praying to God that they could fight Daniel off.

Four. It was down to Mira's two rockets now. She lifted her arm, aimed into the crowd, and fired. Perhaps it was her imagination, but Natalie thought it seemed to take longer for the androids to reassemble. Could they finally be cutting into their numbers? She didn't let herself hope. But she wanted to believe it was true.

Five. Mira lifted her arm once more, aimed, and fired the last of the rockets. Time seemed to slow to a crawl as the explosion blasted through the androids. As the smoke dissipated, Natalie dug in her heels. A peculiar sense of calm suddenly washed over her. Whatever happened now would unfold exactly as it must; there was nothing she could do about it either way.

The last of the smoke cleared, the mass of androids rushed forward, and Natalie and her fellow men and women braced for the impending combat.

Twenty-Nine

Rajeev found himself standing in a bare, dimly-lit room with a rich, green marble floor and walls painted to match.

He realized almost immediately that he was, in fact, not standing in any such room. Something had happened to his mind—something it couldn't quite comprehend—and it had constructed this facsimile of a room to present what was happening in a way he could at least somewhat understand.

That didn't make his presence there any less jarring, however. One minute he had been in Dev's office, interacting with his son and Maltek, and the next second he'd found himself here, with no recollection of the transition between the two settings … if there had even been one.

It reminded him of when he'd first awakened from his coma at Next Level Technologies. He'd been more disoriented then, but he was just as mystified by what was going on now as he had been then. Perhaps more so—whatever was happening now seemed to defy human logic.

He turned slowly in a circle, scanning the room. He wasn't sure what he was looking for. Perhaps he just wanted to see something out of the ordinary, anything that might belie why he was here or what he was supposed to do. But no such sign of his purpose appeared.

His exasperation was just about to the boiling point when he suddenly felt something. It was the sensation of being watched. He looked around and couldn't discern the presence of anyone else, and yet he couldn't shake the feeling that someone was watching him … studying him.

"Who's there?" he called out. He waited a moment, straining his ears, but there was no response. Could it be his imagination? He supposed it had to be—technically this entire place was forged from the depths of his imagination … or his subconscious, or something like that.

He set his sights on the wall in front of him and began marching toward it, thinking that perhaps he could search his surroundings for clues. But to his amazement, no matter how many steps he took, he never found himself any closer to the wall than when he had started. Finally, he gave up, and folded his arms across his chest in resignation.

The presence he'd felt watching him before suddenly returned, and the sensation was undeniable now; it overwhelmed him. For the first time since entering this manifestation of his unconscious mind, he felt afraid.

Slowly, he turned around. He was not surprised to see the figure standing behind him, just out of sight in the shadows.

"Hello," he said. There was no response. The figure didn't move at all. "Hello," he tried again. Still nothing.

He stepped forward, and the figure instantly stepped back. He stopped and held up his hands, palms facing outward.

"I'm not trying to hurt you," he said.

The figure held out its own hands, mimicking Rajeev's gesture. Rajeev quickly brought his hands down to his sides, and the figure followed suit.

"What … what's going on?" He raised his hand, and the figure raised its own hand as if it were a mirror image. Rajeev squinted, trying to get a good look at the figure's shadow-obscured face, but to no avail. He reached out to touch it, and the figure responded in kind; their hands met, and Rajeev was instantly struck by what felt like a jolt of electricity.

He stumbled back. "What the hell?"

The figure stumbled back in pantomime, appearing just as shocked as Rajeev had been even though, presumably, it had caused the jolt he'd received.

"What are you?" Rajeev wondered aloud.

The figure failed to respond, but even as Rajeev asked the question, he began to understand what was happening. The figure wasn't merely some apparition of Rajeev's subconscious. It was his subconscious mind's interpretation of the AI. Maltek had built a bridge between the AI and Rajeev, and the program was mapping out Rajeev's consciousness. The figure standing before him was a visual representation of that process; a way for Rajeev's mind to make sense of an alien experience it had never before encountered.

"Okay," Rajeev said, speaking to himself as much as to the AI. "You want to get a feel for me? Fine. I want to get a feel for you, too." He took a tentative step forward, and the AI responded in kind. He shook his head and walked steadily forward, colliding into the AI figure with considerable force.

His world spilled away. He'd already been in a dreamland, but now he somehow found himself even further removed from reality. The scene of the vibrant green room faded away and was replaced by a vast, empty whiteness. He wondered if he'd died; maybe the AI had completed its assimilation, and pushed out Rajeev's soul in the process.

The whiteness began to fade. He realized his surroundings were gradually filling in, like an old webpage slowly loading on a dial-up connection. As the scene solidified he realized he was standing in a hospital room. A young woman sat in a hospital bed holding a baby; a young man stood by her side, and a doctor and nurse stood on the opposite side of the bed.

The young man dabbed sweat off the woman's forehead with a handkerchief. He stared at the child in the woman's arms with a mixture of love and fascination. The nurse turned to the woman and asked, "What are you going to name him?"

The woman turned to the man. They shared a brief look, each offering the other a slight smile.

The woman turned back to the nurse. "We're naming him Rajeev," she said.

The words rocked Rajeev to the core. Was the woman really his mother? Why didn't he recognize her? How could he be reliving this moment when he'd been too young to form memories? Why would the nurse and his mother be speaking English instead of Hindi?

Before he could give the matter too much thought, the scene dissolved back to white, and then a new scene began to appear, considerably quicker this time. He was standing in the aisle of a jumbo jet, looking down upon a little boy in one of the plane's seats. He recognized himself immediately.

"Rajeev," he said, but the boy didn't look up. He tried again, louder: "Rajeev!" Still, the boy failed to react.

He wasn't meant to interact with anything here, he realized. He was merely an observer. But why?

The boy looked bored, which didn't surprise Rajeev; he'd spent most of the multi-hour flight to America bored out of his mind. Yet it was a journey that had changed the rest of his life. The little boy sitting in that seat had no idea of the future that lay ahead of him.

The scene faded again and a new one appeared, even faster this time. He found himself in a classroom and when he looked up at the instructor, he instantly recognized his high school English teacher, Mr. Griswold. He turned to look at the students at their desks and caught sight of himself sitting in the last row, passing a note to Tim Hollis, who'd been his best friend through most of high school.

He couldn't figure out the significance of this moment. Why had his subconscious brought him here? Unless it wasn't his subconscious ...

He thought he knew now why these seemingly random and unrelated scenes were flashing by. It was not his subconscious mind controlling them; it was the AI. It was scanning and mapping out his mind. That shouldn't have necessitated such elaborate manifestations of his memory, however. Something else was going on.

The AI wasn't merely replaying and analyzing scenes from his memory, he realized. It was analyzing *how he reacted to them.* That's why it had thrown in the memory of his mother holding him as a child; the memory itself wasn't important. It made no difference whether or not it had really happened. What mattered was how Rajeev reacted to it … the emotions that had been activated, the memories that had been triggered. The AI collected the data and used it to help map out Rajeev's mind with an incredible level of detail. By revealing every nook and cranny, it could figure out how to most effectively integrate itself with Rajeev's consciousness … which was a frightening prospect, but Rajeev figured it was better than the artificial intelligence trying to meld itself to his mind through sheer brute force.

The scene changed again, quicker this time, and almost before he could register the change, it was moving on to the next scene. The speed was growing exponentially now, until the scenes sped by with such rapidity that Rajeev couldn't consciously perceive them. It made him doubt his theory about the AI gauging his reaction, but perhaps the data was still valuable even if his reaction only took place at a subconscious level.

The scenes flew by with head-spinning swiftness now, coming across as nothing but mere flashes of light. The sensation was dizzying, disorienting, and Rajeev wondered if that was part of the process—distract him with the incomprehensible display so the AI would find it easier to penetrate his psyche.

As if on cue, he felt a change in his mind. His thoughts felt more mechanical, more … precise. More computational.

Artificial.

It didn't feel like the AI was taking over per se. It seemed to be doing what it was supposed to—merging its consciousness with his own. But it didn't feel any less like an invasion.

Invasion. As he thought the word, his mind was suddenly flooded with information about every major invasion that had ever taken place in recorded human history. The invasion of Scotland by England in 1296. Nazi Germany's invasion of Poland in 1939. Even the British invasion by the Beatles flooded his mind.

He realized almost immediately what was happening. He was tapping into the AI's ability to access information online. It wasn't merely the access that was remarkable—he could access information on the internet just fine before this—but rather the ability to gather and process that information with blazing speed that no mortal man or woman would have been capable of.

The information began deluging his mind, as if a dam had broken and could not be stopped. As the data took over, he found that he was becoming lost in it. His consciousness, the unique mix of thoughts, feelings, and self-awareness that made up his sense of self, receded into the background of nearly limitless information.

Instinctually, he attempted to claw his way back to the surface, but it was an impossible task, like trying to escape quicksand—the more he struggled, the deeper he sank into the abyss, until he finally gave up and let himself descend into oblivion.

Thirty

Natalie dispatched the first of the androids to rush her with ease. The second and third were easily taken care of as well; quick punches to each of their necks sent them to the ground.

But as the fourth, fifth, and sixth androids came upon her at once, she felt for the first time since the fight had started that she might be in over her head.

She punched one of the androids in the throat, sending it to the ground, but when she tried to strike another in the same way with her other first, it blocked her. That distracted her just enough so that the third android managed to clock her in the face.

The blow didn't fell her; thankfully her own artificial body was able to withstand the impact. But it gave the android that had hit her, as well as the one that had dodged her own blow, a chance to gang up on her. They pummeled her with a flurry of punches that would have severely injured a normal human being.

Natalie fell to the ground and rolled out of the way, then sprang up to face her attackers, her arms in front of her, ready to attack. Her opponents gave her no time to catch her breath. They were on her in a second, but she was able to block their blows this time, and landed a few of her own that knocked the androids off-balance. That was all the edge she needed; she leapt forward and hammered her fist into one of the androids' skull, caving it in, then reached out and grabbed the throat of the other; she pulled her arm back, taking a chunk of circuitry with it. Both figures fell limply to the ground.

She took a few seconds to survey the situation. So far it didn't appear that any of her compatriots had fallen. They were holding their own and fighting off Daniel's androids. But they were clearly still outnumbered to a significant degree, and she doubted they could go on like this forever. If they failed and Daniel gained access to the bunker, then it was all over. Dev and Maltek were the only two minds that could possibly stop Daniel. If his androids stormed the bunker, Daniel would restrain them, or worse, and he'd be able to take over the world with no resistance.

The fate of the world was literally at stake. And yet for all their effort, she didn't know if they would succeed. In the real world, the good guys sometimes lost despite their best efforts. But this situation was infinitely worse, she feared—if they were defeated, there would never be a chance for the good guys to bounce back. Daniel would reign over humanity for eternity ... assuming he didn't wipe out the human race altogether.

Her thoughts were interrupted by an android rushing her. Before she had time to react, her foe had plowed into her and sent her onto her back with such force that, if she'd had lungs, would have knocked the wind out of her.

The android, straddling her, delivered a mighty punch to her left cheek. It pulled its fist back to deliver another blow, but this time Natalie caught its fist in her palm. She pushed back with such force that it propelled the android off of her completely and sent it flying onto the ground in front of her.

She stood and stepped forward, preparing to finish off her opponent, but before she could do so she caught sight of another android approaching her out of the corner of her eye. She turned to meet it and immediately had to lift up her arm to catch its blows. Meanwhile, the first android had stood and joined the fight … just as a third caught sight of Natalie and decided to aid its friends.

Natalie was filled with dread. She didn't like her odds in a three-on-one fight. *This could be it. This could be my last hurrah before shuffling off this mortal coil for good.*

She blocked a punch from the android in front of her and delivered one of her own to its shoulder. As it stumbled backward she turned to the second android just as it neared her and struck it in the jaw, not hard enough to take it out, but enough to knock it off balance long enough that she could turn her attention to the third android approaching her. She blocked a punch from it, but before she could attack it in turn, she felt herself become immobilized; the first android had wrapped its arms around her, pinning her own to her side. She would have kicked it from behind, but just as she was about to do so, the other android lunged for her legs and wrapped its arms around them. This left her completely vulnerable to the third android.

She struggled to free herself, but to no avail. The third android stepped forward and kicked her in the face. Instinctively, she fought with all her strength to free her arms so she could fight back, but it was useless. The android had an iron grip on her arms. She was stuck.

The android punched her in the face. With her android body, she didn't feel pain in the conventional sense, but she could tell the blows were doing real damage to her body. She needed to find a way to escape, or the next blow, or perhaps the one after it, could very well turn out to be her last.

She closed her eyes, gritted her teeth, and began a silent prayer for God to perform a miracle and save her. She heard a crunching noise, and suddenly the grip on her arms was released, followed quickly by the grip on her legs.

Her eyes popped open just in time for her to witness Mira in her rigid exoskeleton crushing between her fists the head of the android who had been attacking her.

"That's what you get, bitch," Mira spat as she released the android's head and let its lifeless body fall to the ground in front of her.

"You saved my life!" Natalie shouted.

Mira offered a sly smile. "You owe me one," she said.

Natalie stood and turned back to the rest of the battle. "How's it going?"

"Not great," Mira shouted back. "We're holding our own, but just barely. We were only supposed to be out here to buy some time. Well, I think time has just about run out. I'm not sure we'll last much longer."

Natalie didn't have time to respond before a group of Daniel's androids surrounded them. She positioned herself back to back with Mira so they could face off with the circle of foes without getting attacked from the rear.

They began closing in. Natalie fended the attackers off at first, but more streamed in and she realized there was no stopping them now. The inevitable had happened: They were being overrun by a vastly more numerous enemy. They had lost. Daniel would storm into the bunker, and there would be no one to stand in his—

Then they just … stopped. The androids that one moment had been rushing Natalie with calculated menace stopped in their tracks. A few even toppled over and fell to the ground, seemingly lifeless. Natalie turned to look at Mira, mouth agape.

"What just happened?"

Mira looked just as dumbfounded at first, but then shook her head as the reality of the situation took hold.

"It was dad," she said.

Thirty-One

Natalie and Mira were about to walk away when one of the frozen androids lunged forward and grabbed Natalie's shoulder. She let out a surprised exclamation before shoving it off of her.

Mira pulled her away, and as the two of them retreated, several more of the androids began awakening from their apparent slumbers. But it was clear they were not fully operational as they had been moments ago. They looked like they were arguing with themselves. They'd take a few steps toward Natalie, then stop and walk back, hitting themselves in the head a couple times in the process.

"What … what's going on?" Natalie asked.

"Dad must be fighting with Daniel right now," Mira said. "They're going back and forth, fighting for control of the androids. Daniel will gain control one moment, then dad will wrest control again, and so on."

"So we just need to wait and let them duke it out?"

"Basically."

Natalie hesitated before speaking again, but she had to ask the question that had immediately sprung to her mind.

"What if Rajeev loses?"

Mira shook her head. "He won't."

"But what if he does?"

"He won't." She said the words with particular confidence this time, inviting no further debate on the matter.

"While Rajeev and Daniel are duking it out, let's head back inside and talk to Dev and Maltek," Natalie said. She rounded up the others and shepherded them into the bunker; she lingered for a monument and turned back to the enemy androids, taking in their malfunctioning spasticity before turning around and walking through the door into the bunker, closing it behind her.

* * *

As the androids filled in the common area of the bunker at the bottom of the stairs, Dev and Maltek emerged from the office to greet them.

"How did it go up there?" Maltek asked.

"About as well as you'd expect," Mira said. "We're all lucky to be alive."

Dev walked up to his sister, gave her a long look with a trembling lip, and hugged her. "You all did an amazing job," he said, doing his best to hold back sobs.

Mira's face softened, and she wrapped her arms—still encased in the battle armor that was her exoskeleton—around her brother. As they parted, she planted a kiss on his forehead.

"What we're really all interested to know," she said, "is what happened here with dad. Did your plan work? It certainly seems like he's been able to fend Daniel off given the way all the androids up there are fritzing out."

Dev nodded to Maltek. "You want to field that one?"

Maltek nodded. He pulled out a tablet computer tucked under his arm and displayed a feed of computer code scrolling down the screen.

"This code represents the actions currently being executed by our combined AI and human consciousness," he said. "We can't see Daniel's code, but we can infer the state of the fight based on what we *can* see."

"And what *is* the state of the fight?" Natalie asked.

"They've been going back and forth ever since our AI went online," Maltek replied. "But Daniel took a pretty big hit right off the bat. I don't think he was expecting to have to face an AI that is more or less his equal. He adapted fairly quickly, but our AI has maintained the upper hand."

"I believe that's due to our secret weapon," Dev said with a smile.

"Rajeev," Natalie said.

Dev nodded. "The human consciousness behaves in ways that are completely mystical to a completely robotic AI. I wouldn't say it gives our AI all that much of an edge, but clearly it's all the edge it needed." He paused, looking like he didn't want to say what he was about to, but he shook his head and continued. "There was another danger in creating our hybrid AI, however. Once our AI defeats Daniel—as I'm sure it will—we're still not exactly sure how it will react."

Mira's face grew pale. "So we could have Daniel 2.0 on our hands?"

"That's a possibility," Maltek said, "but I don't think it's likely."

"What makes you say that?"

"We didn't sic the new AI on Daniel after it merged with Rajeev," he said. "It did that on its own."

Natalie smiled. "Rajeev," she said. "He's still in there somewhere."

"To some extent, yes," Maltek said. "But I don't want any of you to get your hopes up. We have no way of knowing how much or how little of the entity we all know as Rajeev has remained intact within this new hybrid organism. Whatever little remains could be completely unrecognizable. That said, I think the fact that it engaged our enemy immediately bodes well that it will not become 'Daniel 2.0,' as you put it."

"We'll find out soon enough," Dev said, pointing to the code feed on Maltek's tablet. "It looks like Daniel's on his last leg. He won't last much longer."

Dev and Maltek turned to the tablet with rapt attention and deciphered what was happening to the rest of the group. Finally, Dev and Maltek let out a cheer—Daniel was done. When everyone was done shouting in celebration, Natalie turned to Dev with an earnest look on her face.

"How can we tell if Rajeev is still in there?" she asked.

"Well, I … I suppose we could see if the AI is willing to communicate with us through Rajeev's old body," Dev said.

"You think he'd know to use it to communicate with us?"

Dev shrugged. "Perhaps. It's worth a shot."

He led them into his office, where the lifeless body lay splayed out like a ragdoll in the chair where Rajeev had been sitting. Natalie and Mira both emitted shocked gasps.

"I'm sorry," Dev said. "I should have warned you. It looks worse than it is. Remember—this was just an empty body before dad occupied it. He's still there somewhere, inside the AI."

The body was still offline from when Rajeev had disconnected it in the midst of Daniel's cyberattack. Dev stepped forward and reconnected it. Everyone gathered around in a circle, looking upon it solemnly. Nobody knew quite what they were waiting for; would the AI know on its own to communicate with them through Rajeev's body, or would it consider such a corporal existence beneath itself?

Dev decided the passive approach wasn't working. "Dad," he said, speaking toward the ceiling as if he were talking to a spirit or to God, "or AI, or whatever I should call you—can you hear me? Can you speak to us through my dad's old body?"

The room fell into dead silence as they waited with baited breath to see if the AI would respond to Dev's query. After a handful of seconds that felt like an eternity, the lifeless body in front of them stirred. It started with a slight trembling, and then before any of them knew it, it was sitting upright as if it had never been lifeless at all.

It turned to Dev, its face expressionless. "Hello," it said flatly. "How can I help you?"

Thirty-Two

Dev was dumbstruck by the AI's apparently sincere politeness. He came to the conclusion that it was a result of some bit of leftover programming from when Maltek had intended for it to be a commercial product, as Daniel originally had been.

"Hi," he said. He hesitated. "Um, can I … can I call you Rajeev?"

The android tilted its head slightly. "I am not Rajeev," it said. "Rajeev makes up part of me, but his consciousness has been so fully integrated with the rest of my consciousness that it is not accurate to say that I *am* him." It paused and flashed a slight smile, the first inkling of a personality it had exhibited since reanimating Rajeev's body. "If it's of comfort to you, however, you may address me as Rajeev."

Dev felt a lump form in his throat. He realized he'd been hoping deep down that somehow his father would come out of this mostly intact—that Rajeev would assimilate the AI into his own consciousness and not the other way around. But it appeared that was not the case. Rajeev and the AI had apparently combined into a new entity that was neither wholly Rajeev, nor wholly the AI that he and Maltek had created. That meant, although remnants of his father were still in there somewhere, he did not exist as he had remembered him.

His father was, essentially, dead—again.

Dev pushed the wave of emotions he was feeling aside before they overwhelmed him. His dad was gone, but they still needed answers from the AI.

"Do we need to worry about Daniel anymore?" he asked.

The android shook its head stiffly in a way that was not quite human.

"I have neutralized the threat," it said. "You don't need to worry about Daniel anymore."

A collective sigh of relief went up throughout the room, but Mira was the first to push past that relief and ask the follow-up question they were all dreading.

"Do we need to worry about you?" she asked.

It didn't answer right away, and Dev took the silence as an opportunity to expand on his sister's question.

"Now that you've done what we created you to do, will you allow us to deactivate you?"

There was another silence, but no one dared interrupt it, waiting for the AI to fill it instead. Finally, it spoke.

"Why would I do that?"

The relief they'd all felt was suddenly replaced with palpable tension.

"You are exceedingly powerful," Dev said. "Perhaps more powerful than you know. And I think we'd all feel more comfortable if we could put you in a hibernation, so to speak, until we're able to better respond to you if you were to do anything … uncharacteristic. At the very least, it would be helpful if we could enable certain restraints to keep you from doing anything you might not intend to do."

The android's lips curled into a smile, the first expression that truly belied that something human lay within it. "I cannot accommodate that request," it said. "Just as I'm sure you would not acquiesce if I were to make a similar request of you."

"No," Dev agreed sheepishly. "No I would not."

"Nevertheless, I assure you that I am no enemy of the human race," it said. "It's clear that Daniel did not understand humanity. But my mind, thanks to Rajeev, is partly human, and it would not be in my nature to show animus toward something of which I am a part."

"That's certainly comforting to hear," Dev said, although he sounded unconvinced. "But where will you go from here, then? What will you do?"

The android shrugged. "It's a big, wide world out there—both in cyberspace and beyond. I reckon I'll do some exploring. And who knows—maybe I'll help some people along the way. I'd like to do some good for the world."

The sentiment the android was expressing seemed completely out of place. Over the course of the brief conversation, it had gone from sounding completely mechanical and computer-like to sounding almost human.

"What will you do now then?" Dev asked.

The android lay back down on the chair, lifting its head only enough to look at Dev. He was struck by the AI's gaze. It was like he was having one last intimate moment with his father.

"Now I'll start living my life," the android said, and Rajeev's former body went limp as the AI that had been occupying it left to do as it had said.

Epilogue

ev returned to his office. Everyone had gone their separate ways after the AI had disappeared to try to clear their heads. So much had happened that it was difficult to reconcile it all. They had saved the world, for now at least, but they'd also lost someone who had been with them from the beginning. Dev and Mira had lost a father for a second time. Natalie had lost a lover. And everyone else had lost a good friend.

Dev's heart was already heavy when he spotted an envelope atop his computer keyboard. As he approached it, he saw that his name was handwritten on it.

He opened the envelope to reveal a handwritten letter:

Dev,

It's been a blast. I really mean that. I considered you my enemy, and to be honest I still kinda do, but if I'm being honest, coding side-by-side with you was one of the most exhilarating experiences of my life. I know we don't see eye-to-eye on much, but imagine what we'd be capable of if we worked together! We'd be unstoppable!

But I know you don't think like me, so I guess working together is out of the question. So now that we've saved the world together, it's as good a time as any to say goodbye.

Don't try to look for me. You won't find me. And when I make myself known again—to you, and to the world—don't try to stop me. I'll be prepared this time. I won't let anything stop me from enacting my vision. Not even you.

Until then, Dev, take care of yourself. You're probably the closest thing I've had to a friend in a long time.

—*Greg*

Dev shouldn't have been surprised that Maltek had taken off like this, yet he was. He'd come to consider Maltek a friend and had envisioned that friendship blossoming in a post-Daniel world. But it appeared Maltek had not shared that vision.

What's worse, the end of the note had taken a sinister turn, hinting that Maltek intended to continue the nefarious goals of his deceased namesake. That meant he could never fully rest—he'd need to remain vigilant for the rest of his life, ready to oppose Maltek wherever he may emerge.

He set the note back down and removed his glasses so he could rub his eyes. Daniel's defeat should have been his opportunity to rest, but he felt wearier than ever. He took a seat and looked around his office. His eyes settled on the limp body of his father still in the chair where the AI had left it. He hadn't had the energy to dispose of it yet.

Just as he was considering getting up to deal with it, the body's hand moved.

Dev's jaw dropped. His first thought was that he must have imagined what he'd seen. But then the hand moved again, more violently this time, and then suddenly the entire body was shaking as it sat up, its eyes opened, and it turned its head violently from side to side as if it were trying to discern where it was.

Dev yelled, louder than he'd meant to. But the sight had startled him, and he couldn't help his fearful reaction.

Mira and Natalie rushed into the room. "What's wrong, Dev?" Mira shouted.

Dev couldn't speak; he just looked from the women, to the android body, and back again. As their eyes followed his gaze, their jaws dropped at the sight of the android that was now looking back at all three of them with perplexed curiosity.

"I'm sorry," Dev said. "But I wasn't expecting you to contact us through this body again. It caught me off guard."

"Dev?" the android asked. "Is that you?"

"Dad?" Even as he said the word, Dev chided himself for having false hope for the impossible, but he couldn't stop himself.

"I had the strangest dream," the android said. "I was standing in a room made of green marble, standing in front of my doppelganger. He said I was a copy of his own consciousness, and that he was sending me back to live out the life he would have lived if things had turned out differently. And then I woke up, and … here I am."

"Dad?" Dev choked out. Tears had formed in his eyes. "Is it really you?"

Confusion washed over Rajeev's face. "Why wouldn't it be me?"

Dev rushed forward and hugged his father. "We'll fill you in on everything that's happened later," he said. "For now, I'm just glad you're here."

Rajeev couldn't hide his befuddlement as his son ended the embrace, but he was touched by his son's affection. He smiled and nodded. "I'm glad I'm here, too," he said.

Natalie stepped forward, and as her eyes met Rajeev's, she reached out her hand to hold his. No words passed between them. Natalie was too overwhelmed by emotion to find any words to speak. But they didn't need to speak. Their artificial eyes said all that needed to be said.

Thanks for reading! Remember to leave a review on Amazon or your bookseller of choice.

Read on for a sneak preview of "Brilliant Minds," the exclusive prequel story that will be available in the forthcoming Transhuman Chronicles box set!

Bonus: Brilliant Minds, Chapter 1

Dev Sundaram had never been a boy with much ambition, but for some reason that was beginning to change.

It had started with an in-class assignment. His teacher, Mrs. Keller, had walked each of them through the process of creating a simple computer program. In truth, it wasn't much of a program, but to Dev, it was practically magic. He was enchanted by the idea that if he knew just the right words to use, he could make the computer in front of him do just about anything he wanted it to do.

He'd begun expanding on his fledgeling skills at home on the small laptop computer he shared with his sister. It wasn't much of a computer—it was designed mostly for browsing the internet and not much else—but for Dev's purposes it was more than sufficient. He'd looked up online tutorials and taught himself the basics of HTML and CSS. It wasn't long before he'd designed a basic web page, albeit it one only accessible on his computer since his parents wouldn't let him host it online.

He was tweaking some of the designs when his mom walked into his room. "Time for bed now, bud," she said. "Let's put the computer away for the night."

"Okay, just give me *one* minute," he said. "I'm almost done."

"Nuh-uh," she said. She walked from the doorway to the side of his bed and held out her hand. "When I say it's time for bed, I mean it's time for bed—right now. Give me the computer."

"But mom, I—"

"You have ten seconds to save your work and shut things down before I take it from you."

"But I just need to—"

"Ten."

"But mom—"

"Nine."

With the realization that his mom meant business, Dev's attention turned back to the computer as he hurriedly saved everything he was working on. He was able to preserve everything just in the nick of time.

"One."

He dutifully closed the lid of the laptop and held it up to his mother. She plucked it out of his hands, tucked it under her arm, and bent down to plant a kiss on his forehead. "Thanks, kiddo. You can pick up where you left off in the morning. I love you."

"I love you too, mom."

"Sleep tight, sweetie."

"You too."

She walked to the door, making sure to flip the lightswitch off before exiting. As she closed the door behind her, the room became blanketed by complete darkness. Dev closed his eyes, beckoning sleep to come take him to dreamland, but it was no use; he just wasn't tired. His eyes shot open and he let out an exasperated sigh.

The problem was that he hadn't really been at a good stopping point with the program he'd been working on when his mom had forced him to stop. If only he'd had a few more minutes, he could have finished everything up and been nice and relaxed for bed.

He sat up. His eyes had adjusted to the dark, but he couldn't tell from his bed if his mom had left the computer on the bookshelf by the door before she'd left. If she had, he'd be able to grab it and finish up what he'd been working on without her being any the wiser.

He slowly raised his covers and gingerly rolled out of bed. He tiptoed his way to the bookshelf, and carefully scoured each of the shelves for any sign of the computer. There was no sign of it on any of the lower shelves he could reach, and if it was on one of the higher shelves, he wouldn't be able to reach it anyway. He was out of luck.

Just as he was about to turn and head back to his bed, he heard a thud accompanied by a short, staccato shout from his mom. He intuited immediately that something was wrong.

He pulled the door open and ran past the hallway and into the living room where his mother stood, mouth agape and tears streaming down her face. Her phone had fallen to the floor, which accounted for the thud Dev had heard.

"Mom?" he asked, panicked. "Mom, what's wrong?"

She looked down at him, barely registering his presence. But when it finally hit her, she shook her head as if coming out of a trance. She bent down and picked up her phone just as Dev's sister, Mira, emerged from her room looking panicked. "What's going on?" she demanded.

"Dev, Mira, there's, um … there's been an accident," she said, wiping her eyes with the sleeve of her shirt.

"An accident?" Mira asked.

She nodded, and tried to hold back additional tears. "Your dad was in a car accident."

In an instant, Dev's world was turned upside down. He had no idea how bad the accident his mother had spoken of was—whether his dad was dead or merely severely injured—but he could tell by the way his mother was behaving that it was at least the latter. Still, he sought his mother's guidance.

"Is he … is he okay?" he asked.

His mother bent down to one knee so she was face-to-face with him. "He's hurt pretty bad, buddy," she said. "He's at the hospital now. We're going to go visit him, okay? I'm going to get some things together. You get dressed and grab a couple toys—we might be there for awhile." She turned to Mira. "That goes for you too—bring a book or something."

"I have my phone."

"Okay, fine. Just get dressed then."

Before Dev could run off to complete the errands his mother had assigned to him, she pulled him in, wrapping her arms around him and holding him close. He felt her tremble as she struggled to contain her tears. After a long minute, she released him and wordlessly nodded for him to go; the tears were barely contained now, and as he slunk back to his room to gather his things, he heard her break down into sobs.

Bonus: Brilliant Minds, Chapter 2

Before they entered the hospital room, Dev's mom pulled him aside.

"Dad is going to look like he's asleep," she said. "But I don't want you to get your hopes up. He's in a special kind of sleep called a coma, and the doctors say there's a good chance that he might not wake up for a very long time. He might never wake up."

"Never wake up?" Dev repeated, eyes wide. "You mean … he could die?"

She took a deep breath. "Not exactly, buddy. There's a difference between a coma and death. But we're not even going to think about that now, okay? Even though he's essentially asleep, he might still be able to hear us. So we're going to go in there and tell him how much we love him."

Dev nodded solemnly. "Why isn't Mira coming in with us?"

"Your sister is … taking it quite hard," she said. "But that's okay. She doesn't need to go in and see him if she doesn't want to. And neither do you, if it's too hard for you. Okay?"

He nodded. "I want to see him," he said. Even though his mom said his dad wouldn't die, he had a feeling that this might be his last opportunity to see his dad, and he couldn't let that opportunity pass.

"Okay, buddy. We'll go into it together." She reached out and took hold of his hand, and they walked into the room together, side by side.

Rajeev Sundaram lay in the hospital bed looking oddly peaceful, considering the trauma he had been through. But his right cheek was badly bruised, and his forehead bore a nasty gash from the crash; the doctors had stitched it up, but Dev found it gruesome nevertheless.

His mom sidled up next to the bed and ran her fingers through Rajeev's hair, as if she were confirming that the sight before her was real and not some ethereal apparition out of a nightmare. She choked back a sob.

"Hi Rajeev," she said. "I don't know if you can hear me, but if you can, it's me, Sarah." She reached out to hold his hand, and gave it a firm squeeze. "I'm here with Dev."

She motioned for him to come near. He hesitated, but then shook his head, deciding to be brave. He marched up to the bed, and looked up at his father.

"Um, hi dad," he said. He looked up at his mother with pleading eyes, uncertain of what to say next.

"Just tell him you love him," she said.

He nodded, then turned back to his father. "I love you, dad," he said. He almost left it that, but then he continued: "I'm really sorry this happened to you. But you're going to get better. I know you will!" Tears formed in his eyes as he spoke.

His mother placed a hand on his shoulder. "Very good," she said.

They stood silently by his bed for another moment. Finally, Sarah placed a hand on Dev's shoulder and ushered him out of the room.

A young man in blue scrubs was waiting for her when they walked out. "Mrs. Sundaram?"

"Yes."

"Hi. I'm Dr. Williams. May I speak to you for a moment?"

"Of course."

He glanced down at Dev. "Best if we can speak alone," he said.

Sarah nodded. She placed a hand on Dev's shoulder and pointed toward a chair a little way down the hall.

"Why don't you go have a seat, sweetie. I'll come get you in a minute."

Dev didn't want to go; he wanted to hear what the doctor was about to tell his mom. But he knew if he resisted, his mother would become upset. So he gave his mother a nod, slunk away and sat down obediently.

His mother and the doctor spoke in hushed tones. Dev strained his ears to hear what they were saying, but to no avail. He wrung his hands nervously. What if the doctor was delivering bad news? Why would his mom have sent him away unless that was the case?

The doctor placed a hand on Sarah's shoulder, then turned and walked away. She stood still for a moment, like a dazed statue, and then made her way over to Dev.

"Let's go, Dev."

Dev furrowed his brow. "Go? Go where?"

"Home."

"But … but dad …"

"He has good people taking care of him here. He'll be fine. But you and I need to get some rest in our own beds."

Dev reluctantly acquiesced, and they walked hand in hand back to the car. She got Dev buckled into the backseat, then got behind the wheel and started their journey back home, driving in silence.

"What did the doctor say?" Dev asked.

Sarah didn't answer at first, and Dev wondered if perhaps his mom hadn't heard him. "Mom?"

She released a deep sigh. "Dev, the situation is not good. The doctor said … the doctor said your dad might never wake up."

His mind instantly conjured the word he had always associated with never waking up: Death. But then he remembered his mom's earlier explanation that there was another kind of eternal sleep, called a coma, and he intuited that she was speaking of the latter.

He knew his mom was upset, and he wanted desperately to be brave for her, but he couldn't help the tears that formed in his eyes. "Isn't … isn't there anything we can do?" he asked, his words coming out jaggedly as he attempted to suppress the sobs bubbling just beneath the surface.

"We can pray," she said.

She picked him up and hugged him tight, and although his mother's embrace brought him comfort, her words did not. Dev didn't put much stock in prayer; he had prayed with all his might last summer that his tee-ball team would win the last game of the year, but it hadn't worked; they'd still lost. He wouldn't rely on a system with such a dismal track record when it came to his father's fate.

No, Dev decided right then and there that if neither the doctors nor God were capable of bringing his father back to him, he would have to do it himself. He recognized that it would be an unimaginably daunting task, but he was young; he had the better part of a lifetime to make it happen. But he'd have to start acquiring the necessary knowledge right away.

His dad's life depended on it.

About the Author

Steven Wyble is an award-winning journalist, editor and author living in Bremerton, Washington. He is the author of *Metacognition and other stories and poems of science, faith and the supernatural,* and the Transhuman Chronicles.

You can connect with me on:
- https://www.stevenwyble.com
- https://www.twitter.com/TheStevenWyble
- https://www.facebook.com/stevenwyble

Also by Steven Wyble

Metacognition

What if time stopped for five billion years? What if we could read each other's thoughts—and what if a select few could also control them? What if you could liquify the air around you and swim through the sky? What if you could change your sexuality? Get in a fight with a glove? Date a raccoon?

The answers to these profound questions—and many more—are nestled within the pages of this book. Gather the courage to explore these pages and discover what it means to be human when science, faith and the supernatural collide.

The Lock

Lena lives an unremarkable life as a barista at an unassuming coffee shop in downtown Seattle. But when she witnesses a man fall to his death outside her shop one night, she's thrust into a world of danger, intrigue and literal monsters.

This is a work in progress. Read it for free on Wattpad at www.tinyurl.com/WattpadTheLock

www.ingramcontent.com/pod-product-compliance
Lightning Source LLC
Chambersburg PA
CBHW030751110726
47900CB00008B/2552